JINGLE BELL FLING

SCARLETT COLE

Published By: Kadelo Group Ltd.

Edited by: Isabel Ngo

Cover design by Letitia Hasser at RBA Design

E-book ISBN: 978-1-7392843-7-4

Paperback ISBN: 978-1-7392843-8-1

To Rachel Hamilton

For always being there.

INTRODUCTION

This is a pure Christmas holiday novella. It has all the Christmas references. Candy Canes, Christmas movies. Christmas Crackers. Even Twiglets. And it also has oodles of forced proximity and steam.

Content Warning/Spoiler:

To be sensitive to readers, I will also note that the epilogue only involves having children as part of the story. I say this not to spoil the HEA, but ensure everyone is comfortable with it before they dive in as this can be triggering for some.

1

PRESLEY

"Fuck Christmas."

Multi-millionaire Hollywood A-lister, Presley James, muttered as he watched the limo drive away, leaving him in the dark and deserted lane with his hastily packed suitcase and backpack.

He was over the fake frivolity, tinsel, and eye-watering light shows. Had been for decades. First, there was the year he broke his leg Christmas morning playing on his new BMX. He'd attempted a stunt drop off the wall outside St. Mary's Church in Totnes, Devon, and had laid there for ten minutes crying until his friend had called his dad to come and get him. They'd both missed Christmas dinner while waiting for an x-ray and had survived on chocolate bars from a vending machine.

Then there was the year his parents had a huge fight that had started with there being no Brussels sprouts in Tesco on Christmas Eve and had ended with his dad leaving his plate of turkey and trimmings to go to his mate's house on Christmas Day. He'd never come home.

Oh, and there was the Christmas his girlfriend had

dumped him on the same day his best friend had gone to Thailand for two weeks, leaving him alone for the holidays with just his mum for company.

And this Christmas was shaping up to be a doozy. With only three days until the big event, he would certainly still be the star of the news headlines come Christmas morning. The fact the headlines were salacious was the least of his worries. Of all the emotions, embarrassment he could handle. Detonating everything he'd been working towards, however, was devastating.

Yeah. Christmas sucked. He'd asked the driver to turn off the Christmas music piped through the speakers, but the crap songs played on repeat, with puke-fest levels of nostalgia and shit lyrics about a mystic big guy in a red suit.

Frost crunched beneath his feet as he walked down the footpath, and he wished he could see the treacherous ground he was walking on. But beneath a pitch black, new moon sky, the banks of the Llangollen Canal in Wales were invisible.

Presley's breath emerged in white puffs, and it was cold enough to freeze the balls off a bull, but all he could do was stride on, dragging his extra-large suitcase behind him and tugging his backpack further over his shoulder until he found what he was looking for.

Salvation.

The only place he could hide out in the whole world without a hope of being found, even if it didn't have a postcode.

A private jet from the States listed under a shell company name and a discrete limo service, with a driver paid well enough to not reveal his location, helped quell some of the rising panic. How could he have been so stupid?

Los Angeles had pulled him in and sucked him dry.

Literally and proverbially. And the whole world was about to find just how badly he'd fucked up.

The fact there were photos?

Jesus.

What a spiral.

"In one smooth move, you've obliterated how your fans see you," his agent, Narmin, had said as he'd messily rolled his jeans and shoved them into his luggage. But she'd also assured him that actors had survived worse in the past, and there was little she wouldn't do in the name of damage limitation for her biggest client.

His fingers and nose ached with the sting of cold. If only the person he hoped to find lived in an actual house, he'd be there by now. Instead, his phone had said—before it died—he needed to make his way to the old Bryn Howel hotel, hit the canal bank, find Bridge 38, and keep walking.

A bitter wind whipped at his cheeks, adding the decision to travel in a hoodie and his leather jacket to his list of regrettable life choices. It had been balmy in LA when he'd left his fourteen thousand square foot home in the flats of Beverly Hills, just north of the famous Santa Monica Boulevard.

His only thought had been to get out of LA. Out of America. And back to the safety of home. Except he couldn't face his mum. Not yet. He could imagine the lecture he was going to get from her. And Totnes, Devon, wasn't where his best friend lived anymore. Midflight, he'd changed his plans from going to see his mum to seeing the one person supportive enough to care about him, the one person who would support him despite the upcoming news.

As he rounded the corner, he found what he was looking for. And solitary green-and-gold canal boat, trimmed in fairy lights, glowing like a beacon in a storm.

There was a small Christmas tree wrapped in red tinsel that fluttered furiously on the bow, and he wanted to punch the thing off into the frigid depths of the murky canal.

He stepped on board and hammered on the door. "Open up, Nova. It's me."

While he waited for her to open the curtains that blocked his view through narrow glass doors, he muscled his case over the bow, where he placed it on his frozen trainer-covered toe. "Motherfucker," he muttered before banging on the door. "Nov. Come on. It's Pres."

A light flicked on inside, its brightness seeping around the edge of the curtains until they were ripped open by a furious-looking sea witch. Fiery red curls framed bright blue eyes. Muffled angry words fell from full lips as she unlocked the doors to her boat, named *Majestic*, and glared.

"What the hell, Presley? First, you scared the shit out of me. Second, it's two in the morning. Third, it's—"

"Fucking freezing. Back up, Nov, and let me in."

She thankfully did as he said as she tugged a thick fleece dressing gown around her before pushing the masses of red curls over her shoulders. And as much as he hated to admit it, just seeing her—furious with him, wrapped in an ugly brown robe—made some of his panic and anxiety ease.

He ducked his head to step inside, then dragged his case down the two narrow steps into the boat, and almost fell face-first onto her bed as he navigated the small space. A cheery warmth greeted him as she closed the door behind him and whipped the curtains closed. After placing his case and backpack on the floor, he was relieved to find he could stand up inside.

Barely.

When he turned to face her, she flung her arms around his neck and hugged him close. "Stop staying away so long."

He grinned, wrapping his arms around her tiny frame. "I've offered to pay for flights to come see me a thousand times."

"Meh."

Like he'd always done, given their foot-and-a-half height difference, he lifted her off the ground and stood up straight, her feet dangling around his shins. She was lighter than he remembered. Or maybe he was stronger. He'd recently finished filming the third gruelling instalment in an action series that had required some severe bulking up. "You were the only place I wanted to come to."

She smelled like sandalwood and fresh air. A third-generation hippie, she came by the vibe naturally. Her nomadic parents had been nineteen when they'd had her. She'd celebrated her first Full Moon Party in Ko Pha-Ngan at fourteen weeks old. Learned to meditate in Goa, India, aged three. Finally, in a bid to give their daughter a traditional English education, they'd settled in Totnes, Devon. She'd become his next-door neighbour, classmate, and best friend ever since. Her parents had left her to her own devices once she'd gone to university to study creative writing. She and Presley had a good relationship and talked all the time, just rarely in the same country, let alone room.

Or boat.

"How did you know where I was?"

Now he had to admit a secret he'd kept for years. "You shared your location with me."

"When?"

"Two years ago, when you were in LA. You were worried you'd get lost and I might need to find you." He didn't add that it gave him comfort, sometimes, to see her on his maps app. He'd worried earlier in the year when she'd moved onto her canal boat, and it had reassured him to see her moving along the canal network.

"I'm always happy to see you but why are you here?"

Now he *was* here, the last bit of energy that had fuelled him the past twenty-four hours expired, and he put her down. "Can we chat in the morning? It's a long conversation, I'm knackered, and I could really do with some sleep." Plus, he didn't feel like baring his soul when he was so tired and already felt disembodied.

"Of course." She turned and led him down the exceptionally narrow corridor. "I'll give you the full tour in the morning."

He smirked as they walked through the middle of the bathroom. "That should take all of five minutes."

"Don't be mean. *Majestic* has hidden depths, like all women."

And didn't he know a thing or two about hidden depths.

The living area was lit by the glow of a slowly dying fire. Not enough light to see the rest of the boat, but the warmth and darkness made him yawn. "We'll set up a proper bed tomorrow if you are staying then. But for tonight, just use this."

She tossed a spare pillow and three thick blankets on the armless sofa, then tugged a strap beneath it to pull it out into a sofa bed. He'd probably fit diagonally, but right now, he didn't give a shit. It was a flat surface with more support than the floor.

"It's perfect, Nov."

He sat down on the sofa and began to unlace his trainers when he noticed they were covered in mud. "Shit, I think I might have made a mess of the floor."

Nova shrugged. "In that case, you can mop the floor in

the morning. Assuming you've remembered how." Her grin told him she was teasing.

A cleaner had been one of the very first things he'd hired after his breakout role at nineteen, ten years ago. He'd planned to go to uni and study drama, but Narmin, his agent, had seen an amateur dramatic play he'd been in. Three weeks later, he'd been cast in his first big-budget movie. "I'm pretty certain it's like riding a bike."

"I seem to recall you broke your leg riding one of those. It's not a high bar." Laughter followed her into what looked like a kitchen area. He heard a cupboard door close and a tap. She returned with a glass of water that she perched on a small side table. "I let the fire die down over night, but it should be enough warmth while you fall asleep. You need anything else?"

Presley looked at Nova, studied her carefully, the girl who'd always been there, and rather worryingly felt . . . something more. Her asking him if he needed anything shouldn't make his heart drop, should it?

He shook his head. To her *and* to the question rattling about in his brain. "I'm good."

2

NOVA

The following morning, twenty-nine-year-old Nova Williams stretched her hands over her head, then pulled the short curtain away from the narrow boat window. Condensation gathered at the bottom of the glass, but it looked as though it was another beautiful crisp morning outside. Frost iced the window and the beige fronds of bracken on the other side of the bank. Three ducks swam by, and she made a note to take a crust of bread to the stern with her.

Mornings on the canal boat always had a happy rhythm to them. These days, she'd pull on some layers and her ugly fleece-lined slippers. Then she'd open the curtains all the way down the boat and follow that by filling the kettle and setting it to boil. She'd then hustle to the engine and, once it started up, would turn the heating on. Then she'd step out onto the stern to get logs and kindling for the fire. In the winter, the stern was protected by something called a pram cover, a tented canopy, giving her somewhere to store her bike and wood for the fire. It also protected her from the elements on the days when she had to change moorings, based on how long the Canal & River Trust allowed her to stay. She'd only arrived in this spot two days ago, so she didn't need to worry about moving for another twelve days.

With the fire stoked and the heating on, she'd make a cup of tea in her "this is what an awesome editor looks like" mug sent by one of her authors. A bowl of hearty oatmeal, topped with berries and a liberal sprinkling of dark chocolate chips, was consumed before she'd even think about her copyediting work for the day.

Given she'd just had her toilet tank pumped out and her water tank filled, with the goal of not moving until the New Year, she was all set to enjoy Christmas. Decorating her miniature world had been joyful. Finding tiny treasures to brighten her space had occupied many a solitary evening in November. Vintage baubles mixed with Scandinavian wood.

Biting the bullet to clamber from beneath the warmth of her bedding into the cold boat, she placed her feet on the floor and saw muddy footprints.

Presley.

Her heart skipped a beat, which was . . . odd.

She'd awarded him best friend status the day he'd put a tadpole in Julia Hodson's water bottle in year one because Julia had made mean comments about Nova's hair and freckles. Their friendship had grown because she was happy to play supporting parts in Presley's imaginary games and plays, He would always be the hero, naturally, where she'd played everything from the heroine to be rescued or the villain to be killed. Once, she'd played a log, sleeping on the floor while he repeatedly dove over her into a death roll.

She'd seen him do the same move, arguably with more finesse, in a movie he'd been paid three million dollars for.

But the sight of his muddy footprints had her thinking of other roles they could play together as adults. Those thoughts had crept in every time they'd video-chatted over the last few months. It was just a phase, she reminded herself. It would pass.

It always did.

Their friendship was the most important one she had. Hell, it was one of the only ones she had, and she wasn't screwing it up for passing flickers of attraction.

Quickly, she grabbed her dressing gown, discarding the thoughts as nothing more than tiredness from being woken in the wee hours. As silently as she could manage, she crept through the bathroom to the living room where she found Minerva, her black cat, curled up on Presley's rising and falling blanket-covered chest.

"Min," she hissed, urging the cat to get down.

Minerva opened one eye, glanced at her, then closed it again, fully intent on ignoring the instruction.

Nova rolled her eyes and stepped into the kitchen to fill the silver kettle before turning on the gas. Once it was cheerfully warming the water, she grabbed a slice of bread before starting the engine and turning on the heating. The boat rumbled noisily to life beneath her feet.

She unlocked the rear doors, bracing for the chill that hit when she pushed them open, and climbed up the steps to the back of the boat. Quickly, she ripped the bread apart, throwing it in the direction of the grateful ducks who splashed and squawked playfully as they attacked it.

Using the basket she left at the stern, she filled it with kindling, small branches, and larger logs. When she stepped back inside, she nearly dropped the entire thing.

A practically naked Presley stood in the middle of the living area. Well-defined muscles disappeared beneath boxer briefs that clung to his hips like a second skin. His waist-to-shoulder ratio seemed to be superhuman. And certainly it was wrong she wanted to lick the distance between his belly button and waistband, right? His dark hair stood up in all directions as he tried to wrestle a blanket off the bed and wrap it around himself.

"So, you still look like that, huh?" she said in the absence of any smarter comments as she closed the doors. She'd been cruising the Kennet and Avon Canal when the first movie in the *Battle for Earth* series had come out. The cinema in Bath had been showing it and she bought a ticket. But it felt weird to watch her best friend on screen with two hundred other people who didn't know him. Especially as he'd already offered to send her a ticket to the opening night red carpet thing, and let his glam squad be hers too. She'd turned him down, not wanting him to spend his money on her. That wasn't what their friendship was about. Neither did she want the publicity that came with being on his arm, friend or not.

But it had also been the first time she'd watch him make out on film. Where she'd seen the curve of his very fine bum undulating beneath strategically placed white cotton. Where she'd watched him cup another woman's cheeks, kissing her tenderly, with heat in his gaze, and she wondered what it would feel like to make out with him. To make out with her best friend.

"Like what?" Presley said, looking down at his body. He ran his hand over his stomach, which was more solid bank of abs than the squishy pooch she had. Cheese, a crisp white wine, and an insatiable love of any kind of red fizzy sweet weren't conducive to a body like his.

She stepped past him toward the fire, placed the basket down, and gestured up and down his body. "The whole 'I'm a superhero, hear me roar' thing."

Presley burst out laughing. "It won't last long. I just

finished filming; I don't need to look like this again for another four months."

"It should be annoying that you can just turn it on and turn it off again."

"Anyway, what the hell was that black thing? And that noise?" he asked, bleary eyed, as she gathered her wits. Wits that had scattered all over her boat's wooden floor at the sight of him. At his words, the kettle began to whistle loudly.

"And why is everything on this boat so goddamn violent?"

"Tea?" she asked, hurrying to turn it off.

"Please."

"The black thing is my Christmas present," she said, busying herself making two mugs of steaming hot tea. "I adopted her last week and she's a gift to myself. I called her Minerva, after the famous female escape artist. I was starting to think she didn't like people; she's been avoiding me since she got here. But she seemed to like you just fine, so maybe it's just me she doesn't like. The noise is the boat. The heating doesn't work without the engine running. I turn it on in the morning to get some hot water and heat in the radiators. And the whistle was just the kettle."

As she spoke, Presley busied himself in his case, finding a pair of joggers and a hoodie which he pulled on before adding socks. By the time she handed him his mug, he was dressed.

"Sorry. I really like your boat. And your cat." They both looked over to where Minerva was now making herself comfortable in the warmth of his blankets. "It's all very you."

"Thank you." Having the parents she did, she'd been looking after her own shit for as long as she could remember, and loved the independence she'd created, in both her life and where she lived. Her canal boat allowed her to be nomadic while never leaving home.

They slipped into opposite sides of the four-seater dinette, their feet awkwardly dancing with each other beneath the table as they got comfortable.

"It's lovely to see you, Presley. And you know you can stay as long as you want to. But why are you here?"

Presley mindlessly rotated the cup on the table, then sighed. He flopped back on the dinette and ran a hand over the stubble over his chin. "I fucked up. I did something so unbelievably stupid I can't even think about it."

"Mate, we've all done stupid shit. Do you remember the time I tried to run up that escalator the wrong way in that shopping centre in Plymouth while drunk and fell? At least a hundred people witnessed that."

"I wish that was all it was."

Nova picked up her mug and took a sip, the hot liquid easing her throat that was suddenly dry. "Just say it."

Presley looked at her across the table and she could see the shame and embarrassment in his hazel eyes. "I fucked my co-star's twenty-year-old daughter while high."

She bit back the sudden feeling of envy, shocked by its appearance, and focused on her friend. "Okay. Bit young. Probably beyond healthy given you have to work with your co-star for the press junkets, but it doesn't sound too terrible."

"No. But the part where it became a threesome with her college roommate does. And the part where I passed out and the two of them took photographs is. The Hollywood gossip is already saying how I'm the biggest douchebag in the history of movies and how my future contracts are at risk. Honestly, I was lonely, felt isolated, had a frustrating day, and I allowed my ego to get the better of me. I allowed her to buoy me along, thinking it would be a fun night. But now I feel like it was a setup. I'm not the guy out there trying to ruin the reputation of my co-star's daughter by enticing her into a threesome, yet that's how the narrative is playing out. It's devastating."

Nova's jaw dropped. She wasn't even sure what she could say that would make even a modicum of difference to the situation. "That's a lot to unpack."

Presley pushed his cup away and laid his head on his arms on the table. "I'd just fucking made it, Nov. I can't even tell you why I did it. It's like the third time in my entire life I've smoked weed. The first two were while we were still in high school." He sat up again, his body unusually agitated versus his usual laid-back self. "We were sequestered in this place in Alaska towards the end. The weather was frigid. The filming was brutal. And Mario Bianchi's daughter and her friend came to visit. We're all at the same hotel, nothing grand, more quaint. And I'm at the bar, mad about how the day had gone, and they suggest we go back to Sofia's room to smoke some weed so I can wind down. Seemed like a great fucking idea because I hadn't been sleeping. Weed. Proximity. Not to be crude, Nova, but I'd not had sex in like three weeks. They were both hot. Italian. I'm high." Presley slides his hands into his hair and tugs hard. "Now they've sold the images to some gossip site and I'm about to get toasted. Hell, it's probably already done. My phone died last night, and I couldn't face charging the damn thing."

It was obviously wrong that the only thing Nova really remembered from the whole monologue was that it had been three weeks since he'd had sex, but she tried to shift the now awkward thought from her brain.

"Won't it all blow over?"

Presley sighed. "It will. I know. But the damage is already

done. I was about to make a shift. I've been typecast as an action hero. I've always loved acting, and I really wanted the chance to experiment with my range. And I wanted to work on movies with important messages. I've been putting myself forward for those kinds of roles, even saying I'll take a huge pay cut to do them. It's not like I need the money. But every time they'd say no, that they couldn't see it. But there's a movie that's about to be announced. Oscar-winning director Hattie Lee is directing. And I managed to convince her I could do it. Just. It was between me and another actor. They were about to announce the casting yesterday, but they pulled the announcement. Hattie is worried. The story is about the rape of a female naval officer on active duty in a war zone. I'd play her lawyer. Hattie is worried about the optics. She's going to fire me. I can feel it."

"It's awful they can fire you over your personal life. But I also can see it from her perspective."

Presley pressed his palms to his face. "That's the worst part. I can too. And it's taken years to get this far, Nov. Years."

"Let me check if it's hit," she said, fishing over the back of the dinette for the kitchen counter where she'd plugged in her phone.

She entered his name into the search bar and then . . .

Oh, shit.

"How bad is it?" Presley asked.

Nova winced and shook her head. "It really depends on how you view things."

"Not helping, Nov."

"Well, on a positive note—for a guy, I would assume—they're now calling you Subway."

Presley leaned forward. "Subway?"

"Because Sofia said you were a foot long."

3

PRESLEY

"Like the Subway foot-long sandwich?"

Nova nodded, and then laughed nervously. "It's a compliment on your . . . erm, manhood, I guess."

"Jesus. It's big, but it's not that big." Anger bubbled up inside. "Sorry, Nov. That's TMI. I know. I've built a family friendly platform. I don't even have any tattoos, even though I love them. I just want to be taken seriously as a fucking actor and be given a role I can show my range in. All of this ruins all my efforts. A sex scandal, nude photos, and drugs."

"It was just weed. It's not like you were freebasing cocaine."

"If I issue a statement saying it was just this once, everyone will roll their eyes and say *sure* in the way that says they don't believe you." He picked up his tea and drank it while Nova continued to scroll. "What else is there?"

"Do you want to see?" She offered him her phone, and there was just enough time to see a picture of him on the bed, his dick pixelated out. "Fuck. No." He shoved it away.

Nova placed her phone on the table and reached for his

hand. He let her take it. "It'll pass, Presley. It always does. There was that celebrity couple suing each other this year, remember the one that was on TV every day. People forget."

"But studios don't. Neither of them have announced major film deals since. Didn't you notice?"

Nova shook her head. "I didn't. You want to stay here until it all blows over?"

"Do you mind? Mum wasn't expecting me home, so she was going to my uncle's for Christmas. I'll need to give her a heads-up though, in case the paparazzi manage to track her down. Shit, I don't want to tell her."

"Sally will be cool."

"Would *you* want to call *your* mum and tell her your bits are out all over the internet because you got high and fucked two strangers?"

Nova shrugs. "I'm pretty sure that without the extra person, that's exactly how I was conceived."

"Funny."

"Funny, but true. You forget I was born nine months after they met at in an ashram during a gap year."

He *had* forgotten that little detail. "Anyway, this whole thing sucks."

Nova tapped the table with the nail of her forefinger, then wiggled out of the dinette bench seat. "Here's the thing. It's done. You can't go back in time and not think with your dick, no matter how long it is."

"Nov," he warned.

"Sorry. Couldn't resist. But it's done. All of it. The only thing that matters now is how you ride the storm. How are you going to face it? With wisdom, temperance, courage, or justice?"

"Such a good little stoic."

"I'm serious." Nova grabbed his shoulders and shook

him as much as she could in the small space. "Let's go for courage and a pinch of justice. For courage, you can stay here, and we'll have an awesome Christmas. You're not hiding, you are just waiting for general interest in the story to dissipate."

Presley rolled his eyes. "Wow. Sounds like so much fun." Yeah, his tone was sarcastic.

"Oh, stop. Then we'll also go with justice. Can't your PR team do damage limitation? Or your agent? Or manger? Or whoever all those people you pay an exorbitant sum of money to flock around you are?"

"I should charge my phone in case I've missed calls and stuff."

"Yes. Proactive action. And while you are checking your phone, I'll make food. How hungry are you?"

"I feel sick to be honest."

"Pah. Sick wasn't an option. I have oatmeal and this awesome list of Christmas toppings."

"Why does Christmas have to invade oatmeal?"

Nova folded her arms across her chest. A chest he was suddenly more appreciative of than he'd ever been before. "Because it's Christmas. I have gingerbread and walnut, apple and cranberry with cinnamon, and peppermint brownie."

Presley winced. "That last one sounds grim."

Nova's eyes lit up. "Yes, but it comes dressed with a candy cane, and you can never have too many of those."

And that was another thing he hated about Christmas. Peppermint candy canes that just went sticky in your hand and stuck to your teeth. "I'll pass. Can I just get it plain or with a banana and peanut butter on top? It'll tide me over until we go shopping."

"I have food."

"I know. But I eat like four thousand calories a day, and I don't expect you to pay for that, seeing I just dropped in on you." He could see the battle of wills she was having with herself. It bugged him that she wouldn't take anything from him. Said she didn't want to be beholden or something. A fancy word given her job was to edit them all day. "It's just food, Nov. We'll get a ride to a big Tesco."

"Fine. We'll stock up seeing there are two of us to feed now. Go make your call. I was going to start the fire, but I'll wait until we get back from shopping." She placed her hand on the radiator. "I'll turn the engine off now these are hot."

Presley looked over at his phone with dread. "How about while you turn the engine off, I'll plug my phone in, and then you can give me the tour first?"

"I smell a stalling gesture, but because I love my baby so much, I'll show you. Meet me at the stern when you're done."

"You realise the stern is like fifteen feet away and I can see you from anywhere in this room." He reached into his bag, rummaged around for his phone and cable, then looked for a socket.

"Oh, shut up. And you can charge your phone by the TV over there." She waited for him to plug it in then led him to the back of the boat where she switched the engine off. "Okay. So, stop me if I tell you stuff I already showed you when I was renovating it."

"I will," he said, knowing full well he wouldn't, because she was right. He absolutely was stalling.

"Ready? This is a fifty-eight-foot—so it can go through just about every lock in Britain—semi-traditional stern—which refers to the size and shape of the deck outside—reverse layout—which means the kitchen is at the back instead of the bedroom—canal boat."

Presley leaned against the kitchen counter. "You've practised that, haven't you?"

"I have. Did I nail it?"

He nodded. "You did."

"Good. So, there are bench seats outside, then we have this little utility area with space for coats and muddy shoes on one side, storage under the steps, and a cupboard with the inverter charger and circuit board and ignition blah, blah, blah. Then on the other side we have . . ." Nova waved jazz hands in the air as she opened two narrow doors with mirrored panels on them.

"What's so special?"

Her face looked at him as if to say *duh.* "I have a combination washing machine and tumble drier."

"That doesn't feel like the flex you think it is."

Nova shook her head. "You know nothing, Presley James. Having one of these on a boat is a big deal. Otherwise you're stuck going to the laundrette. Although, I still tend to do that occasionally. When the laundry gets too piled up, I'll take four loads in giant blue IKEA bags to the closest place. It's all done in a couple of hours. Anyway, I digress. This is the galley. She's nine feet long."

He looked around the kitchen properly for the first time. The top half of the walls was painted white, and ash-coloured wood graced the bottom. There was a three-burner hob on a white countertop and teal-blue cupboards below. "The kitchen is way bigger than I thought given your crap photography skills."

Nova slapped his arm, and he grinned. "Stop, or I won't show you my surprise."

When she smiled at him, talking about showing him her surprise, his mind went in a completely different direction.

Jesus Christ.

Having sex on the brain was what had gotten him into this whole mess. And that must be why his brain was misfiring when it came to Nova. He'd been stuck in Alaska filming, and beside the one night with Sofia and her friend, whose name he couldn't even remember anymore, he'd not had sex more than one night in a month now. That was it. For a guy with a high sex drive, it felt like a fucking oasis.

"Show me," he said, his voice a little gruffer than he'd intended, and for a moment he could have sworn he'd seen Nova's pupils flare.

She jumped and then turned to the cupboards opposite the burner hob and pulled down a cupboard door. "I fitted in a slimline dishwasher."

It looked barely wider than a dinner plate, but she was obviously proud of it. "Nice. As is the big sink-and-drainer combo with the tap on the bendy hose thing."

"The dinette turns into a double bed which we could just set up permanently for you, although it's only six feet four, so you might prefer the couch. And there's storage underneath. Oh, and look."

The dinette was on a slightly elevated platform, and Nova bent over, pulling out a drawer that was a wine rack. He gave it a cursory glance before checking out the curve of Nova's dressing-gown-clad butt.

Quickly, he looked away. The drawer had one bottle of white and one bottle of red. And a lot of empty spaces. "You've got a lot of storage packed in here."

"Thank you," she said, standing up again before grabbing her hair and pulling it up into a messy ponytail. And, no, he was not looking at her tits again. The ugly dressing gown had come undone, and he could see the tight fit of her pyjama top revealing perky nipples.

"Living room?" he said quickly.

"Couch on left. TV and fire on the right. It's a tall fireplace because that narrower door on top is a small oven. Saves on gas in winter. I'll throw a chilli or casserole or something in there, and the heat from the fire slow cooks it."

"Clever."

The doorway to the bathroom sat in the middle of the living room wall and against the side of the boat on the bedroom wall, but it was a decent space with a rain shower.

"You need to press the button on the wall there to use the shower, it assists in pumping the water out. And if you can, try to use the shower at the gym and pee outside."

He turned quickly to look at her. "Wait. What? What gym? And why do I need to pee outside?"

"I have to run the engine to run the shower, and fuel isn't cheap."

"I'll pay for the fuel. Next, peeing?"

"It's a pump out toilet tank. You pee in there and we carry it around until I go to a marina and pay someone to pump everything out. It costs like twenty quid."

"Again, I'll pay."

"But then we have to travel to the marina, and we might lose our spot when we come back, and I was planning to stay here until after Christmas."

"The last thing I need is someone accidentally seeing my dick."

Nova laughed. "I think that ship has sailed." Then she paused. "Wait. I'm being horribly insensitive. It's not funny that they took pictures of you without your consent. I'm making fun of something I shouldn't be making fun of. If the tables were reversed and it had been done to a woman by two men, we'd all be outraged. I'm sorry."

Unexpectedly, she pulled him into a hug, and he slid his hands beneath her dressing gown to pull her to him. It felt good to have her close. The last forty-eight hours had been like sailing on a ship in heavy seas. Ups and downs, a feeling of displacement in space. But holding her felt solid.

"When I said pee outside, I didn't mean off the edge of the boat. I meant like, at the gym or the grocery store or whatever."

Her voice was muffled against his chest, and it made him smile. "Got it. Now, show me the rest."

4

NOVA

"You know the shops are open between Christmas and New Year, right?" Nova asked as Presley piled food into the shopping cart she currently pushed towards the fruit and veg aisles.

He pulled his baseball cap down lower over his eyes, tugged the scarf she'd loaned him a little higher up his face, and hunched his shoulders in a bid to keep his anonymity. "Yeah, well. In case you didn't notice, I'm on the front page of that newspaper on the newsstand over there."

She grabbed a box of Christmas crackers off an end display and put them in the shopping trolley. Presley picked them up and put them back on the shelf.

"What are you doing?" she asked.

"We don't need crackers. They're just paper waste filled with tat."

Nova sighed and folded her arms. "We aren't doing this this year."

"What?"

"The I-hate-Christmas schtick, Ebenezer. Don't be a hater. Every year you get moody all over again."

He pulled the trolley over by the bananas and grabbed two bunches. "It's the darkest time of the year, and I'd rather be somewhere sunny."

"So go," she said, even as the words hurt. Had he come to her just because he was desperate rather than because he really wanted to see her? If that was true, she was even more stupid than she thought . . . imagining that the hug in the bathroom meant more than just a hug. "No one is forcing you to be in a supermarket in Cefn Mawr right now."

"That's not what I meant, and you know it. I came here because I couldn't think of a better place to be. But can we admit that winter in Britain is gloomy?"

She took a deep breath. "Fine."

"Honestly, Nov. Santa is just a big man in a suit. All the music sucks. Decorating the house is just a waste of time, given it all has to be put away after. Trees get killed. You eat like you haven't seen food and lose track of what day of the week it is. Just about the only thing that is bearable are the stupid jumpers."

As he spoke, a guy walked by with a jumper that said *Rein-beers*.

Nov raised a hand and placed it on his arm. "But, Santa is all about believing in something. And the music? It unites young and old when we play songs everyone knows and can sing along to together. And the decorating? Those lights add a bit of sparkle and magic to the dark, gloomy nights. I don't have a good argument for chopping down trees beyond getting live ones in pots and replanting them, but tree trimming is a tradition the whole family can do together. And when you've been good for fifty-one weeks of the year, what's wrong with eating a handful more Quality Street than you should? It props up winter and gives the weary a break before it's January and we start all over again."

She led the trolley to the citrus. Might as well grab more of anything hardy that would last, seeing Presley had insisted they get a cab to the store. He'd disappeared into her room for half an hour before they left to handle to messages while she'd made breakfast. Minerva had paced by the door, periodically letting out a long continuous mewl as she anxiously awaited his return to the living room. Nova had killed the time vacuuming the condensation off the windows, building the fire so it would be ready to light when they got home, and checking that the lines to the canal bank were still secure.

When he came back, he'd looked drained and unusually quiet, so she'd let him eat in peace.

"I'll tell you what," she said as he sniffed a mango before adding it to the shopping cart. She reached for his hand and squeezed it. "I'm happy you're here. It's been too long since we just had time together, and it sounds like it's been an age since you had a break from filming. Let's try to make the best of it. Let's cook nice meals. I don't think a turkey would fit in my oven, but we could do nice steaks. And if crackers really offend you that much, we won't get them, but I will play Michael Bublé on Christmas Day whether you like it or not. If we binge, let's buy our favourites and not feel guilty about it, but let's eat two-thirds healthy so I can still eat brie. We can read and do jigsaws and walk along the canal. I'll even let you pay for once without splitting it."

Presley sighed. "Fine. And I'm sorry. I've blown in here with a cloud hanging over me, and I don't want it to hang over us. I mean, you know, you and Christmas and what you had planned."

Us.

Two letters had never sounded so good, but he'd

corrected himself so quickly she wasn't sure what to make of it.

By the time they had finished loading their trolley an hour later, the store was starting to get busy. The cashier had looked at Presley twice, but Nova had been able to tell the moment the cashier convinced herself that there was no way a Hollywood A-lister stood in front of her.

Within ten minutes, they were back with all the bags on the kerb, as close to the canal as they could get.

"Shit," Presley said when countless bags were sprawled in front of them. "I never thought about how we carry them back to the boat."

Nova grinned. "How about you show me what all the training you paid for bought you? I'll stand here and mind the bags until there is just enough left for the two of us to carry them."

He took his hat off his head and plopped it on top of her curls. "Watch and weep, weakling," he said as he grabbed four bags in each hand. He disappeared beneath the bridge, and five minutes later reappeared. "I put them in that tent thing on the stern."

Nova shrugged. "That's perfect."

It took him three more trips before there was a manageable amount for the two of them. "I didn't think about where we are going to put everything," Presley said, as she unlocked the double doors and slid back the roof panel so they could walk down the stairs at full height.

"You'll be surprised at the storage I managed to squeeze in," she said. "Start passing me the bags down."

When they were done, he closed the roof panel and locked the doors back in place. While she dealt with all the fresh items, Presley filled the wine drawer. He'd insisted on a lovely selection of whites and reds and some champagne.

"Did you know I had to find space to put extra batteries just so I could have a bigger fridge? It's why I don't have any skylights too, so I could cover the roof with solar panels. It's only got an icebox-size freezer though."

Presley slid behind her and peered over her shoulder. She could feel his breath on her neck, her own catching as he placed his hand on her hip. Surely they'd touched each other before this way. But it hadn't always left her chest feeling so tight, or her clit so excited.

"I bet it helps though."

His proximity stole her ability to process what he was saying. She took a breath to find her wits. "Yeah. Means I don't need to go shopping so frequently."

He squeezed her hip. "What else can I do?"

It took another half hour to get everything put away. The counter was a little more crowded than she liked with overflowing items, but she noticed Presley had been sneaky. He'd bought things not on his list but that would stock her up. Toilet paper, washing-up liquid, rice, tins of soup.

"How did your mum take it?" she asked when they were seated at the dinette later, finishing their steaming bowls of tomato soup and grilled cheese sandwiches.

Presley looked at the fire. Burnt-orange flames licked the glass, giving the space a warm glow. "She's disappointed. Told me I'm nearly thirty and should know better, but that she loved me anyway."

"Do you think you should tell your dad? I mean, I know he's been—"

"A dick? No, he can rot in hell for all I care."

He'd reappeared shortly after Presley's first multi-million payday had been announced. At first, he'd seemed sincere. But it hadn't taken long for him to start asking for money. When Presley had cut him off, he'd gone to the media and tried to sell stories. The problem was, he didn't really have stories about Presley to tell. So he'd badmouthed Sally for brainwashing Presley against him.

That had been the line.

"Do you need to work this afternoon?" he asked.

Nova shook her head. "Yesterday was my last working day. It's Friday, remember? So, Christmas Eve tomorrow and then Christmas day. I didn't plan on working until New Year."

"Why don't we—" His phone ringing cut off his train of thought, and Nova had never been so interested in the end of a sentence as she was right now. "Sorry, I need to take it. It's my agent."

Nova gave the bowls a quick rinse before putting them in the dishwasher.

"I don't know what else I can tell you that hasn't already been said." Presley paced the living room. "No . . . I can't help how they perceive me . . . Of course I wish the whole thing hadn't happened . . . How long is the hold for?"

The conversation was interspersed with pauses.

"I'm happy to talk with them, give them reassurances. Tell them everything we are doing to get all the details taken down . . . No, I haven't looked . . . How many? Fifty thousand and growing. Maybe you should tell that to the producers then. Set it up. Thanks, Narmin."

Presley tossed his phone on the sofa, slipped back into the dinette, and put both hands on top of his head.

Nova wiped her hands on the towel and walked over to him. "What happened?"

"The hold on the casting announcement still stands for an undetermined period. I just wish the director would speak to me directly instead of through my agent. It feels wrong that I can't just explain."

"You pay these people to give you good advice, Pres. Do you really think they are making the wrong decisions?"

Presley shrugged. "I don't know. My head says they're right, but my gut . . . my heart, says they're wrong. I don't want to do blockbuster action my entire life. I'm fed up with this constant objectification of my body as an asset to be bent at some director's will. And there's this other part of my acting range I want to express."

She threaded a hand through his hair and massaged the back of his neck. His hand slipped around the back of her thigh, and she banked the tingles it caused. "Wisdom, temperance, courage, or justice?"

"Temperance means moderation, right? That's the last thing I feel like. I feel like day drinking until I pass out and can pretend this whole thing didn't happen."

"Then let's do it."

Presley looked up at her. She wasn't sure if he was aware of the way he stroked her skin, pausing occasionally to squeeze her leg. "I was only joking."

"No. I can't remember the last time I just sat on the sofa, watched movies, and drank. It's depressing doing that by yourself on a canal boat."

"Fine, Nov. Let's do it."

5

PRESLEY

"But you picked the last two." Nova looked at him, five hours later, a wry smile on her face.

"I feel like you're taking advantage of me," Presley replied before taking another sip of the Italian Barolo. The twenty-five-pound bottle was a long way from the Barolo in his wine cellar back in LA, but it wasn't awful.

He was ridiculously comfortable. Nova had two footstools that doubled as seating and also had storage inside. He was slumped on the sofa with his feet on one of them. The blanket from inside it was draped over him, and the fire flickered in his peripheral vision. The window behind them was open because the room had gotten too damn hot, creating a cool breeze over his face.

"How am I taking advantage?" she asked, pointing the controller at the TV. Her position mirrored his.

"You lured me in with two action movies so you could use it as leverage to watch this."

"Ah. But those two action movies were just decent. *This* is the greatest movie in its category."

While he had a heady buzz going on, Nova was entering

the drunk phase. The *this* and *is* had slurred together. Never could hold her alcohol. When they'd been younger, he'd taken it upon himself to be her drinking buddy. Whenever they'd gone clubbing together, he'd make sure to take her home as soon as the slur kicked in. When he'd left for Hollywood at twenty, leaving her to fend for herself on a Saturday night had been one of his biggest worries.

But here, in the warmth of her boat, she was safe with him.

"Nov. There is no such thing as a great Christmas movie."

"What?" she said, eyes wide, mouth indignant, as she pretended to stab herself in the heart. "That might be the most sacrilegious take you've had about Christmas yet."

"Just speaking the truth. People watch them because they've been told they're supposed to. And big studios continue to make Christmas movies to capture the Christmas dollars."

"Cynic. I can't wait for you to get a Christmas Day release so I can shit all over you for doing it."

Presley laughed. It was a fair comment. "Okay. Let's hear the pitch for why I should watch this with you."

Nova turned on the seat, glass in hand, to face him. She was close. Close enough that her hair brushed his hand that was resting on the back of the sofa. Her curls were soft, and he had to resist the urge to wrap one of them around his finger.

"It's based on famous Charles Dickens book, which mean it's technically great literature. It stars Michael Caine, legendary actor and all that. Have you met him?"

Presley grinned. "No. But I saw him at a distance at the Oscars last year."

"Huh." By the way her nose turned up at the end, he

could tell Nova was unimpressed.

"I'll try harder to meet him next time. Carry on."

"Okay. So, it also has Muppets and singing, and it's the best Christmas movie ever."

"Sounds shit. But go ahead. I'm getting crisps. Want anything?"

"Twiglets, please."

He grabbed both from the counter and noticed a new message from his agent.

Narmin: *Lining up recovery plan for new year. Encouraged Hattie Lee to see how quickly it blows over. Stay low.*

A part of him was curious exactly what she meant by that. But he understood the last two words. He looked over to where Nova was trying to find their movie. Yeah, he'd made the right call to come here. There was no way she was going to do anything that would cause him any trouble.

Before he sat down, he topped up their wine glasses.

Nova pulled open the tin, and the strangely yeasty smell of the Twiglets hit him. "Don't you think these are another Christmas tradition we don't need?"

Nova laughed. "Doesn't it burn?"

He was confused. "What burn?"

"All the hot takes you've got stored up inside you?" She offered him the tin and he wrinkled his nose in refusal. "It's the novelty of Christmas. Like those giant tins of super thin ginger biscuits you can get from Costco every year. And the giant tub of Quality Street. Advent calendars. Like, what other month of the year are you actively encouraged to eat a chocolate before breakfast?"

As she scrolled through the movies to find the Muppets, one of his own movies appeared. An action special set in an airport on the Fourth of July. Just seeing it brought his ass back to reality with a thump. His heart lurched in his chest and his breathing felt . . . resistance. Like he couldn't breathe deeply enough.

He leaned forward, putting his head in his hands. "I should call Mario, apologise or something."

Nova placed her hand on his back and rub circles. "No offence, Pres, but he should be calling you. Apologising for his douche canoe of a daughter and her friend. Right up until the point when she took photos of you passed out and naked, you were just three consenting adults."

He shook his head. "Can you consent if you are high? Did any of us?"

Nova sighed. "Fair point. Dubious consent can be a thing when alcohol and drugs are involved. But there were two of them and one of you. You weren't the aggressor in all this. You should know I read their original article about it."

"Nov. Why would you do that?"

"Because I wanted to see what their motivations were. They aren't claiming anything dubious. It's the total opposite. That you were some kind of superhero lover with stamina for days. And the original article is filled with highly posed shots of the two of them. I think they were just looking for their fifteen minutes of fame."

Presley leaned back and rubbed his hands over his eyes. "I hate that I know that. I hate that *you* know it."

"I was worried, like you were, that they were going to say it was non-consensual. But they don't. You don't owe Mario an apology. First, it's patriarchal and misogynistic. What those women do and did as consenting adults has nothing to do with their fathers. Second, you are the wronged party. Like I said, up until the point they took photos, you were three consenting adults. As soon as they took that first photograph, you were the one wronged. They owe you an apology."

"For a moment I forgot. I was thinking about Twiglets one minute, and the next, one of my movies appeared as you scrolled, and it all came back."

"Right, stand up," Nova said, jumping to her fuzzy-sock-clad feet and fumbling with her phone.

When the music burst out of the speakers. "Nov. I can't do this."

He bracelets jangled on her wrists as she threw her hands up as much as the low roof would allow. "Eleven-year-old Presley would be very disappointed in you. This was your favourite song."

Shamefully, it had been. If anyone asked what his favourite song was a kid, he'd roll out some vintage Zeppelin song to be cool. But he had loved dancing and bouncing on his bed to Eric Prydz, "Call on Me."

Nova grabbed his wrists, and he let her drag him to his feet. "I'm going to hit something if I start dancing in a boat only marginally wider than my arm span."

She simply shrugged and began to dance. He'd always loved that about her, the way she let music flow through her. Sometimes, when approaching a scene he was dreading, a scene where his nerves were getting in the way of the performance, he'd close his eyes for a second and channel her energy.

"Come on, Pres. No one can see. And you need some happy endorphins."

"I can't do this."

"Then act. I've heard you're pretty good at it."

That one got him to smile. "Fine." He wasn't the greatest dancer. It had been a problem in one of the romantic leads roles he'd played. They'd expected him to waltz. He'd felt the pressure to perform. But here. With Nova. Who'd danced with him since they were in the school play as Reindeer Numbers Three and Four, he just gave in to the escape of it.

Half drunk. Jet-lagged. Overwhelmed. But strangely joyful.

He caught a glance at Nova as he turned. Her hair draped down her back, she bit down on her lower lip while her head was back, eyes closed. How had he never noticed the way her hips flared out and how tight she was around the waist? And her tits looked fucking fantastic.

But more than any of that, he realised he could simply be with her.

By the time the song finished—she'd put the seven-minute version on—they flopped down onto the sofa. And Presley felt immensely better. So much so he grabbed a pillow and threw it against her lap before curling up on the sofa so he could lay his head on her.

"Okay. Put your movie on and let's get it over with," he said.

"We should do that between every movie, have a dance break."

"Don't get carried away."

She pressed play and conducted in the air, waving wildly as she hummed the intro.

And when she was done, as Gonzo and Rizzo the Rat introduced the story, she slid her fingers into his hair. They reached down the back of his neck and massaged, then her nails would trail over his scalp.

It was relaxing.

And arousing.

And somewhere around the time Michael Caine was buying the biggest turkey in town, he realised he'd not felt this happy in a really long time.

6

NOVA

A dull thud in her temple woke Nova from a sleep so deep she could barely keep her eyes open. Her throat was dry, and . . .

There was someone in bed with her.

Not just someone.

Presley.

And his arm was around her, his hand cupping the underside of a breast. And his leg was between hers, with . . . Yup. An erection. Somewhere in the panic was arousal.

Shit.

Did they . . . ?

Her thoughts scattered as she tried to piece together what had happened the previous evening. The Muppets. They'd watched *A Muppet Christmas Carol* while drinking a second bottle of red.

They'd paused at the end and thrown a ready-made lasagne and garlic bread in the oven. Food was probably the only reason she wasn't puking right now. Unless she already did last night.

Then she'd persuaded him to watch the first *Nativity*

movie. And once he'd got past the fact it starred Martin Freeman who he'd admired as Dr. Watson in *Sherlock*, Presley had actually laughed at the antics of Mr. Poppy and the children.

Had she seen the ending?

Did they open a third bottle?

Crap. There wasn't enough milk thistle in the world to help her liver if they had.

She glanced down beneath the gap in the covers of the bed. The T-shirt she'd worn the previous day was on, but her bra had obviously been removed. God, she hoped she still had her panties on and—

"Stop thinking, Nov," Presley said gruffly against her ear. "Until we get out of bed, just forget I'm me and I'll forget you're you."

"But we're friends," she whispered.

"Friends who are hungover and really fucking comfortable. Just go back to sleep, babe."

They'd slept in the same bed before. When she was at university, and he'd come stay with her in the cheap student house in Southsea. They'd camped. Twice. In a postage-stamp-sized tent where they'd had to step outside to give the other privacy to change. But there was something terribly intimate about the way he held her now, the way his body spooned hers.

And she wasn't entirely certain Presley was properly awake. From the way he'd sagged against her after speaking, he'd fallen back to sleep pretty quickly.

He must still be drunk.

Maybe she was.

God, yes. That was why her brain was running a mile a minute. Not the fact her best friend was pressed up against her in only his boxers.

The drumming in her head got worse when she opened her eyes again. So, she closed them, hoping it would make things better.

He'd called her *babe*.

How could things feel better after that?

But somehow, she managed to doze off again.

When she woke, Presley was gone. The boat was running, the air felt warm, and the sound of the pump told her Presley was in the shower. As tempting as it was to lay in bed and inspect whatever had happened, she got up, pulled on some comfy clothes, and tied her hair up.

She needed the toilet, but not badly enough that she was going to knock on the door and ask him to get a wiggle on in there. Instead, she unlocked the doors at the front of the boat and hurried around the canal path to the rear of the boat so she could get to the kitchen.

The windows were vacuumed of condensation, the living room tidied of their party debris, and a fire flickered to life in the fireplace.

And the kettle was hot.

Quickly, she made a pot of tea, knowing full well one cup would not be enough that morning.

"Shit," Presley said as he stepped into the living room. "Scared the crap out of me. How did you . . . ?"

He wore a towel, a navy blue one, low on his hips. Water dripped down his chest and she followed a droplet. For a second, she watched it with her cup halfway to her lips. "Sorry, what?"

Presley smiled, the kind where only his mouth seemed to move, but she caught a flash of his dimple.

"I was asking how you got to the kitchen without passing through the bathroom, but in the time it took you to check me out, I figured you'd walked around the outside of the boat."

He rummaged in his case for a moment and, as if on purpose, to goad her raging hormones, he held up navy boxer briefs. "Forgot to get underwear."

When he stepped back into the bathroom, she placed her palm on the kitchen counter and let her head drop. "Get it together, Nova," she muttered.

It had never been like this between them. And perhaps the flirting on his part was part of why he'd ended up in trouble. He'd not had sex for a while, had been flirting with those girls, and now he was here. Maybe this was who he was now. The guy who could have any woman he wanted.

And perhaps losing control of his faculties was what led to this. Weed with those girls. Alcohol with her. Thank God they hadn't slept together in the sexual sense because that would have been—

Incredible.

Reckless.

Unredeemable.

She didn't believe for a millisecond he would deliberately hurt her. But people accidentally hurt each other all the time. Even her parents, who had promised that *this* was the year they'd come home for Christmas, hadn't delivered. Of course, they'd explained, very pragmatically. Ticket prices were high. They'd see her in February for sure.

They'd been the same when they missed her graduation. "*Make sure someone takes a video of it so we don't miss it.*" Presley had recorded the video. He'd flown from Croatia where he was filming a fantasy TV show, stayed for two hours, then turned straight back around to film that night.

Her friends had been transient. For the longest time, she'd not been in one place long enough to make any. Then, when she had started school, they'd made fun of her and her parents' nomadic adventures and the fact she always smelled like the incense her parents likes to burn. Then there had been the awful era her mum had taken up tie-dye, and everything in her closet had been varying shades of rainbow.

Layer on a riot of ginger curls and a love for dead poets, and she was certifiable high school fodder.

But Presley had always been there for her. And the idea that they could screw that up because of alcohol and hormones was terrifying.

Presley walked back into the living room as she poured her tea. His damp hair was brushed back from his face. He'd shaved, and she knew it meant she'd be able to see his dimples more clearly.

"I'm sorry if me being in your bed made you uncomfortable. In hindsight, you seemed uncomfortable when we woke up, and I should have moved right away. But you insisted on another dance break after *Die Hard*."

"We watched *Die Hard*?"

Presley shrugged. "Meh. You stayed awake to shout, "Yippee ki-yay, motherfucker!" then fell asleep and snored all the way through Alan Rickman's demise. But when I woke you up, you suggested a dance break."

"What song did I pick this time?"

"You went all Beyoncé on me. "Crazy in Love" with some squat drops."

"That's why my thighs hurt this morning. I thought I'd slept funny."

"Anyway, you said it was a faff to make up the beds and that given we were both grown-ups, we should both just climb in yours. Being half-cut and too tired to care, I agreed. Anyway, I'm sorry."

That sounded so like her. "Surprised me more than anything," she answered honestly. "I've woken up alone for most of the last year."

"A year? Since you . . . ?" Presley looked at her. "That's quite the drought."

"We aren't talking about my sex life."

"I think we are. That's pitiful, Nova."

"Well, we don't all have a plethora of attractive human beings around us at all times. In case you hadn't noticed, I live along the canal bank and lower the average age by about two decades."

"You know you can set your location on dating apps, right?"

Nova shuddered. "Male privilege suggests that's viable. You wouldn't believe the slurry I saw in my messages when I did that. Honestly, it was pitiful. I have no inclination to do any of the things I've been asked in the past."

Presley playfully body checked her out of the way so he could pour a cup of tea. "Like what?"

"One guy asked if I would be willing to babysit his kid for the day if he had sex with me."

Presley raised an eyebrow. "For real?"

Hmm," she took a sip of tea. "He even clarified that I looked like I needed sex, and sex with him would be so great that it would be worth looking after his kid for a few hours."

"Jesus."

"Yup. There was another who asked if he could come over to mine because his mum was home. And one who said after a date that if he'd known my tits were small, he'd have suggested splitting dinner instead of him paying for it because he didn't really want a second date."

"Jesus. Men are trash."

"They are. Do you want to hear about the guy who asked

if I lived on a farm because he was willing to bet I'd be really good at raising cocks?"

Presley put his hands over his ears. "Stop."

Nova laughed. "You definitely won't like the guy who opened with a multichoice asking if I liked choking, hair pulling, or both."

"Do you? Sorry. Forget that. Tell me you blocked him."

"I deleted the entire app. Call me old-fashioned, but I'd like to meet a guy in a bookstore or a library or over a long spin cycle at the laundrette. But we've got way off topic. I accept your apology, but it really isn't necessary. It's not a stupid idea. Turning the dinette into a bed *is* a lot of a faff, and we are grown-ups." She looked up at him. "Right?"

He held her gaze for a beat longer than normal, and she wasn't sure exactly what she saw in his eyes.

As he blew out a breath, he tapped the end of her nose. "Sure."

She narrowed her gaze at him.

"I'm going to go for a run," he said quickly.

"You just showered."

"Yeah, but I just realised I can't turn up on set in January looking like a Christmas pudding. Will you be okay on your own?"

Hadn't he said he didn't need to be in such good shape for four months? "I always am."

In more ways than one.

7

PRESLEY

Presley fumbled lacing up his trainers.

He needed to get out of there before he did something remarkably stupid.

Like kiss his best friend.

Setting his phone to track his run, he snuck out of the doors at the other end of the boat and hit the canal path running before he could turn around, march back into the canal boat, and lift her up onto the counter before kissing those gorgeous lips off that smart mouth.

Mud squelched beneath his feet.

It was a really bad idea assuming the canal path would be clear. Deep gouges were present in the gravel and they'd filled with water. It was cold to his toes, and he had a feeling he might need to watch out for frost bite. But he was out, allowing his body to take over and do the work to clear his mind.

Kilometre one consisted of huffing in air and the mental reminder that the first kilometre was always the worst.

By kilometre ten, he'd found his groove, one breath for three footsteps, and turned around to head back to the boat.

By kilometre twenty, the boat was back in view and his head was clear.

When he'd left LA, he thought he was running away from the scandal. But the more he thought about it, the more he realised he'd been running to her.

To Nova.

And now that he was here with her, on the tiny shell of a boat she'd made into a home, he knew he didn't want to be anywhere else.

Not because the steel tube floating on frigid water was his preference, but because it was where Nova was. And he'd take her anywhere and anyhow he could get her.

He'd separate his thoughts. All of them. Even the dirty ones.

If he was honest, his feelings for Nova had developed over the last year. He'd date. Often other famous actresses and musicians. Not because he was pretentious, but because those people were friends, friends of friends, and neighbours. One had been intelligent. An actress who was also studying comparative literature at Brown University on the side. But some of the others had been . . . bland. Morphing themselves around him and his likes. Never having an opinion on anything, from where to have dinner to the politics of the country they lived in. Then he'd go home and find himself video chatting with Nova. Just the previous week, she'd asked him why there seemed to be more respect for dead people than the living, and they'd spent two hours dissecting it.

By the time they'd hung up, he still wasn't sure of the answer, but he'd slept like a baby that night.

Then there was the reality that ever since he'd arrived, there'd been . . . tension. Something more to their relationship. A new layer that he was certain Nova felt too. The way she held his gaze, the way she'd stroked his hair, the way they'd curled up against each other and fit so perfectly it was hard to imagine waking up next to someone else ever again.

And, yeah, the accidental boob grab.

Tits were the reason men were the weaker species.

He stepped onto the back of the boat so he could leave his muddy and probably stinky trainers under the tented awning. Mud caked the back of his legs, and he was going to need another shower. When he stepped inside, he called out her name. When she didn't answer, he assumed she was in the bedroom at the other end.

On the dinette table was an open notebook.

A poem of sorts, although it didn't rhyme.

In Nova's handwriting.

All the words I want to say

Tucked between bodies

Where your skin touches mine

So the universe begins.

Happiness and heartbreak

Found in fault lines formed between

Her degree was creative writing, but why did she spend her days copyediting other people's work, when she wrote such beautiful things? He touched his finger to the ink, stroking it softly.

She had a poetic heart.

He tugged his long-sleeved shirt over his head, pushed the door into the bathroom open and—

"Shit, Pres." Nova grabbed the silk gown hanging on the back of the door and draped it around her naked body, tying the belt tight around her narrow waist, but the damage had been done.

There was zero chance he was going to forget her small

but all-natural breasts and the dusky colour of her erect nipples now he'd seen them. Or the smooth curve of her ass. Her foot had been propped on the side of the shower tray as she applied lotion in long lines down her legs.

"Sorry," he said, turning quickly. "Didn't hear the water or pump so assumed you were in the bedroom. And there's a reason door locks were invented you know."

"Fists knocking on wooden panels came first I would suggest. I'm decent now."

When he turned, he realised she wasn't so much decent as the best bits were covered. But the gown was cinched tightly at the waist. And in her haste, she hadn't closed the panels fully, allowing a deep vee at the front that practically hit her navel. The vibrant silk, so different to the ugly brown gown she'd worn the first night, barely clung to the edges of her breasts, which he now really wanted to take into his mouth and suck on.

He thought about the dating apps comments she'd received, the one where the guy had said she was great at raising cocks. His nylon running shorts were probably giving the game away as to exactly how he felt about her.

Immediately, her cheeks went pink, and she glanced towards to frosted porthole window. "How was your run?"

"Helpful." He needed to talk with her about what was going on between the two of them. But now wasn't the time, when he was covered in sweat and mud, and she smelled fresh like citrus.

"Is the back of the boat still unlocked?"

"It is. Although shouldn't you get into the habit of locking it? Especially while you are in the shower." His sudden worry about her on-board safety was another indicator things were shifting between them.

"Did you see a single person on your run?"

"No. Wait, yes, I saw two dog walkers."

"There you go."

"What is that supposed to mean?"

"Dog lovers aren't serial killers. They wouldn't want to go to prison and leave their dogs behind."

"I'd like to see the data on that, Nov."

She smiled at him. In the still steamed-up bathroom, it felt too intimate. Too private. Too special. "I'm fine. You should get showered, I'll get dressed. I had planned to go for a walk this afternoon, and then go to the pub tonight for a drink seeing it's Christmas Eve. You feel up for that? Or is it better to skip the pub?"

He hadn't looked at his phone beyond checking for messages from his agent and manager. As per his request, they were holding back all but the most crucial reports of what was being said. But he'd bet his last pound that they could find a quiet corner in the pub where he could keep his head down. "They both sound great. Give me time to stretch and shower. Perhaps have some lunch, and then we can go."

She placed her hand on his chest directly over his heart. "Take as long as you need. I'm still self-medicating my hangover with tea and digestive biscuits."

He placed his palm over the top of hers and rubbed the back of her hand. Had she ever done something like that before? Was he reading more into her actions? "I'll be ready in about an hour."

After he'd stretched his body, Presley felt better. Perhaps flying through the night and sleeping on her sofa then curled up on her bed had left him tense. But the exercise and lengthening out had reversed it. And for the first time in days, he felt a little more in control of his breathing.

He turned the water for the shower on, then hit the button to start the rhythmic drone of the pump. When he stripped the rest of his muddy clothes and stepped under the spray, he groaned. The small rectangular shower carried her scent. The bottle on the shelf said tangerine and cranberry. He inhaled deeply, knowing that when he hugged her and pressed his nose to her neck, this was what she smelled of.

The erection he'd gotten under control after she'd left the room flared back to life. With his head beneath the hot spray, he palmed himself as his body responded to the stimulation. Long strokes took him to the tip of his already leaking dick, all the way down to his balls. In his mind, visions of Nova began to take shape. Visions of her wrapped up in his life in LA. In a bikini by his pool, drinking with him at Chateau Marmont, on his arm at red carpet premiers and the Oscars. She'd wear a slinky dress, one all straps and no substance, and they'd laugh as he playfully tried to extract her from it at the end of the night.

When the dress slithered to the floor, he'd realise she'd been naked beneath it all night, and he'd pick her up and fuck her against the wall before laying her down in their bed to make love to her for the rest of the night.

His breath came out in a gasp as the images brought him closer to the release he needed.

"Jesus," he muttered beneath his breath, speeding up his strokes until his body hit peak sensitivity. Every stroke felt as though he was one moment away from coming. He did his best to hold it off, to resist, to enjoy every second of sensation, until his body could take it no longer and he came in thick spurts.

His body shook, his knees weak, and he pressed his free hand to the wall to keep his balance in the small space.

But even as his chest sucked in air, his thoughts

remained on her, all her curls on his pillow as they slept, wrapped up in each other's arms.

The image cemented in his mind that somehow, he had to convince Nova to give the two of them a chance, even as he feared he could change their relationship forever.

8

NOVA

"Focus on the normal things," Nova muttered as the bacon sizzled in the pan. "Hangover. Bacon. The need for bread. Cups of tea."

She heard the water and pump switch off in the bathroom and her mind went straight back to Presley. Perhaps more significantly, a very specific part of him that had been happy to get a look at her naked.

The news reports hadn't lied.

Aroused, he was amply proportioned.

Not that she hadn't noticed his junk before. Nylon shorts in summer and grey joggers in winter had given hints of size, but she'd never paid too much attention.

Until now. When there might as well have been a giant sign hanging from her bathroom that said, "Look at Presley's giant erect penis."

"It's just boys being boys," she told the fridge as she reached in to get mayo, tomatoes, and lettuce. He'd told her it had been a while for him due to filming, and now he was getting hot and horny and the idea of an available woman. Not her.

And she was not going to let him ruin the friendship the two of them had, the most precious and valuable relationship there was in her life, over a bonkers urge to procreate.

She chopped the tomatoes while looking out at the canal. There was ice forming against the bank, and she made a note to go out later and crack any that had formed around the hull.

When everything was prepared, she turned to the dinette.

“Shit.” She’d left her notebook out on the table, the one where she jotted poetry ideas down. She’d been doing it for years. Whilst she’d studied creative writing, she realised she didn’t have the commitment to write a full book. Lord knew she’d started several. Great ideas that she could see on bookshelves with great covers. If only she could get past the first twenty thousand words of writing them. It was as if she just ran out of steam or enthusiasm. Or perhaps a better idea came charging into view and she’d change gears in a heartbeat, leaving the other story dangling without completion.

But poetry had become her friend.

It could be written in one line or two pages.

And the notion of identifying the most perfect and precise words to express her feelings was the best part of the challenge. While a story could have up to a hundred thousand words, a tossed salad of ideas and phrases and adverbs, a poem was deliberate.

Sharp.

Concise.

There was a wild beauty and staggeringly clinical technique to it.

Poetry was bold and kind and could cut through vagueness to deliver the most heartfelt of messages in the time it took to change channel on the TV.

She slammed the notebook shut and put it away on the bookshelf across the fire. Her words were private, inept, and a record of her own feelings.

When the door to the bathroom opened, Presley was dressed in jeans and a long-sleeved Henley. She felt prepared to meet him in her jeans and favourite emerald-green sweater.

"Hey," he said quietly, as he stepped into the kitchen.

"I thought BLTs would be a good choice. Bread to soak up alcohol, veggies because health, and bacon because it's delicious." She lifted the bacon out of the pan and laid it out on the kitchen roll she'd prepared to soak up the grease. "It won't take a minute to assemble them and—"

"Look at me, Nov."

There was something so commanding about his voice she couldn't help but put the tongs down and wipe her hands on the tea towel. There was a roughness, a needy edge to his tone, and she knew if she turned to face him, something cataclysmic was about to happen.

But she did as he said anyway. Words wouldn't form.

"You know what I'm about to say, don't you?" he asked.

Nova shook her head. If she denied it, culpability would be all his.

He smiled softly. "You do, babe." He reached out and cupped her cheek gently. "We've been on one track our entire lives, but we're faltering onto another. I really want to change onto those tracks, give in to whatever this is for a little while, see if we've been missing out on something even bigger."

Babe.

Should four letters ever feel so impactful?

"You're just horny," she said, dismissing his words even though she had similar thoughts of her own. "You told me that was how you ended up in this mess in the first place. Sexually frustrated, wrong place, right time, blah, blah, blah." She turned back to the toasted bread and squirted mayonnaise onto each slice, more for Presley because she knew he liked it.

Presley took the bottle out of her hand and placed it on the counter, hemming her in.

Hands appeared on the countertop on either side of her waist. As he buried his nose against the side of her neck, she found herself tilting her head to give him more room. His warm breath made the hairs on the back of her neck and down her arms tingle as they stood on end. "You think that's all this is, Nov?"

When his lips brushed her skin, she shivered. It was a whisper of a touch, more air than anything. His hand wrapped around her waist, tugging her to him. Her head hit his collar bone. At school they'd been called *the odd couple* because of the height difference between them, but they hadn't noticed.

Now, she noticed it every millimetre of it.

The two of them were reflected in the window.

"Tell me you aren't feeling this, and I'll let go," he said. His thumb sneaking beneath the hem of her sweater to stroke her skin softly. "I'll go find a hotel and get my shit together, so we can carry on being friends and you won't hold it against me that I caught feelings for the person who means the most to me in the world."

Nova inhaled slowly. "What if we ruin *us*? What if this is just some weird phase?"

Presley smiled; she felt his lips against her skin. "This didn't start once I climbed on board. It's been growing for a while. Frustrating me even further when you don't let me book you a ticket to come see me more than you do. But we can discuss logistics later. What's it going to be, Nov? You want to carry on making those sandwiches while I go pack, or you want to turn around, tell me you feel this too, and let me kiss you for the first time?"

"I hate the idea we might be throwing a hand grenade into our relationship." Without his friendship, she'd be lost.

But she hated the idea of him leaving even more. Hated it with a passion. And she hated the idea that fear might hold her back from experiencing something truly wonderful.

"Promise me something," she said.

"Anything."

"I need you to promise that this won't end badly. I know you can't promise that it won't ever end. But promise me you won't do anything to make me hate you for the rest of our lives."

He pressed off the counter and placed his hands on her waist, turning her to face him. He held her chin in his fingers. "I promise, Nova. Now tell me."

"I've felt it too," she admitted.

His smile reached his eyes. "Good." His lips touched hers, briefly at first, as if testing the temperature of water. Secure in the fact that the two of them kissing wouldn't cause some fracture in the cosmos, she leaned into him, placing her hands on his hips. "Ready?" he asked.

"For what?"

"This." Presley cupped her cheeks and kissed her again. More firmly this time, his tongue sneaking in to meet hers. Every part of her came alive. Her knees felt weak, her body vibrated with a swirl of energy she couldn't control. Everything coalesced and fused where their lips met.

His hands snaked into her hair, cupping her head, holding her exactly where he needed her. His shoulders rounded so he could reach her.

With no effort at all, he grinned as he lifted her onto the counter, pushing the toast out of the way.

She'd been wrong. There *were* things she didn't know about him. She didn't realise how innately sexual he could be. It was as if a light switch had been flipped, and now she was seeing and feeling him in technicolour. And she definitely had no idea how good his cock would feel through their jeans as he tugged her to the edge of the counter and pressed up against her.

She never wanted it to end. Partly because it felt so good she could barely remember her name, but also, when they did, they would have to face the reality of what they'd just done.

"Nova," he muttered against her lips, the tone filled with more than friendship. It was filled with need.

His hands slid down her arms, over hips, along her thighs and back again, inviting a trail of sensation, before he reached for her hips and squeezed them hard.

When the kiss ceased, he pressed his forehead to hers.

"Does this mean I need to come up with a cute nickname for you?" she whispered.

Presley smiled. Not the one he used when he was on a press junket, but the one he used when he was relaxed and happy. Carefree, even. "You don't have to do anything. Nothing changes."

"Yet, everything changes."

He stepped back and stroked his fingers down the side of her cheek. "You're still the most precious person in the world to me."

"Sweet talker."

"Let's finish making lunch then go out, before I get other ideas on how to spend the afternoon."

"We're really going to do this? I mean, that sounded like a question rather than the statement I intended. But I guess I only just realised exactly what that means."

Was there a plan where you could lose your stomach pooch and go up a cup size in twenty-four hours? If she was going to get naked in front of him, she might have to fast. After the BLT, obviously.

He took her hand and led it down to the outline of his erection through his jeans. "Yeah, I just realised that too."

She snatched her hand away and shook her head. "You are incorrigible."

"I've been called worse. But, yeah, we're doing this. And you aren't going to overthink it."

"Who said I'm overthinking it?"

He raised an eyebrow.

"Fine, I was overthinking it. Now move out of my way so I can finish lunch."

He stole another kiss and a strip of bacon. "Yes, ma'am."

9

PRESLEY

"You smack my hull into the side of the canal, and you will pay to get the whole bottom of my boat blacked and pay to put me up in a hotel while it's in a dry dock," Nova said, sipping on a glass of champagne while occasionally reaching for the tiller to correct his direction.

Presley couldn't help but laugh. "Babe, we're going at two and a half miles per hour right now. How much damage do you think I would do if I drove the boat straight into the canal bank? Worse, what would you do to me?"

She eyed him carefully. "Try it and you'll find out."

After they'd been for a walk, he'd convinced her to move the boat for the night. The stretch she was on had interspersed canal boats, meaning there would be lots of space the following day to come back. But the boy in him had really wanted a try at steering the nearly sixty-foot vessel.

"And don't forget, it pivots in the middle. It's not like steering a car."

"Babe, I've seen faster moving snails. I've got this." Except, he sort of didn't. The front looked an inordinately long way away, but there was no way he was letting Nova know he wasn't as confident as he sounded.

But he was having fun.

The canal became incredibly narrow as they travelled closer to Llangollen. In some places it was only one boat wide. "You hop off and walk ahead," she said. "Call me and tell me if there is a boat coming in the other direction."

"Why don't I steer, and you walk?"

Nova raised an eyebrow. "And leave you to navigate my boat through this narrow section with exactly thirty-seven minutes experience under your belt? Never."

"Fine," he said, tugging the collar of his leather jacket tighter around his neck. "But for the record, you have the warmer winter clothing."

Her laughter rippled over him. "So, jog it, action man."

He did as she said, and before long they were moored up in the visitors' berths next to an electrical supply, which Nova assured him was exceptional. She'd let him park the boat, or dock it, or whatever you did with a canal boat. He'd nudged the concrete edge of the canal, and she'd pursed her lips in warning.

He'd kissed them.

She'd laughed.

The canal was shaded on both sides by tall trees, and when he stepped off the boat to tie it to the bank, he could see out across the centre of Llangollen. With all the fairy lights illuminated along the outside of the boat, it looked welcoming and homely.

And . . . shit . . . Was he suddenly appreciating the joy in it?

Pah.

Once the boat was secured, they ambled down the steps into Llangollen. Nova wrapped her hands around his bicep and snuggled against him while he shoved his hands in his pockets out of the cold wind. “You were right to suggest bringing the boat,” she said. “It would have been really chilly to walk it back tonight.”

“We can grab a cab, you know.”

“Meh. Cabs on Christmas Eve are like triple fare or something.”

He paused on the pavement and turned to face her. “You know, Nov, I get that you have never liked taking stuff from me. And I’ve appreciated it, because I’ve always known that you’re here for me, and not what I have. But if we’re going to make this work, you’re going to need to get comfortable with it. Because I’m more than willing to do long-distance for a while as we figure this shit out, but I’m not prepared to only see you every six months while you save for airfare given I have twenty million to spare.”

Her eyes went wide. “You have twenty million? To spare?”

Laughter bubbled up inside him. “Yeah. I mean, I got paid three, five, and six and a half million just for movies one through three.”

“Shit.”

He kissed her pout because he could. “Yeah. So, if you need your boat blacking, or we want to take a cab, or you feel like a three-day trip to LA just to make out with me, we do it. Right?”

“Can I get used the fact we are kissing, first? Like build up to it?”

He brushed a rogue curl from her forehead. “Sure. If you let me pay for dinner tonight.”

“Fine.”

“And let me give you some cash for fuel and pump out of the toilet tank.”

"Fine."

"And maybe spoil you whenever I want to, seeing I left LA so quickly that your present is still in my library."

"What was it?"

"That would be telling."

He'd tugged his hair beneath a beanie and had pulled the collar of his jacket up around his ears. Nova had loaned him a red-and-black checked scarf, but he decided to stop at the outdoors shop and pick up some warmer and more waterproof clothing. He bought gloves and a thicker hat and threw in an emerald-green fleece he'd caught Nova eying. The stock was limited, but the black waterproof and thick fleece he found would be so much better than freezing his dick off in a leather jacket. Given he'd caught at least three women staring, he decided the whole outdoorsy look would help him blend in better with those around them.

And maybe he could leave them on the hook next to Nova's on the boat when he returned to LA. A visible reminder he would be back.

Nova rolled her eyes when they rejected his black Amex while talking about credit card fees. Fortunately he'd another they accepted.

With his leather and Nova's fleece tucked in a bag, they left the shop. "I can't believe you just dropped five hundred quid without blinking."

"What did I say about money?"

She raised her mittened palms. "I forgot."

"Anyway, I'll give you the fleece tomorrow, and it can be your Christmas present."

"Yay." She slapped her palms mutedly together. "Don't you just love it? The chaos of it? The carols? Everyone busily wrapping up for Christmas, pun intended."

"This is definitely shaping up to the be the best Christmas yet."

They wandered to the old Corn Mill pub and restaurant that looked out over the angry River Dee. It rushed around rocks and foamed. Inside the cosy stone walls hung with pictures and lights and boughs of evergreens, they feasted on grilled sea bass with crab croquettes and braised shoulder of lamb. Nova asked for a glass of champagne, and he bought her a whole bottle. When she attempted to correct his order, he raised an eyebrow and she mimed zipping her lips and throwing away the key.

Yes, he wanted to impress.

As they ate desserts—a tart rhubarb and ginger sponge with custard for him, and a sweet sticky toffee pudding for Nova—he noticed she'd gone quiet.

"You okay over there?" he asked, sipping on the pint of North Star Porter he'd ordered.

When she looked up at him, her cheeks were pink. "I was just thinking."

"About?" Thankfully, the table for two near the old stone window had afforded them some privacy, and Presley had sat with his back to the rest of the room.

Nova looked out of the window and bit gently on her knuckle. He also noticed her fidget in her chair, as if squeezing her thighs together.

Wait, was she . . . ?

"Babe," he cautioned. "What are you thinking about?"

"What happens next."

"In general, or the moment I pay the bill and we walk back to the canal boat?"

"The bit after both of those two things."

Her gaze held his as she bit down on her lip. Leaning

closer to her, he whispered, "Are you thinking about you and me naked?"

"It's impossible not to." Her voice was slightly breathy, and suddenly his dick was ready for the next course.

He raised his hand and looked around at the nearest server. "Can we get the bill please?"

It took six torturous minutes to get and pay the bill, two minutes to pull on their layers, and five minutes more to hurry back to the boat. Nova shook as she tried to get the keys into the lock, Presley banged his head stepping inside because he was too busy looking at her ass.

They both kicked off their shoes in the mudroom area, then dropped the rest of their things as they peeled their clothes off each other's bodies on the way to the bedroom. He should be a gentleman. Offer to turn on the heating for a little while or start the fire. But he couldn't take his hands off Nova's warm body or his lips off her mouth.

It was Nova who realised that while it was dark in boat, they should still close the curtains.

Plus, he wanted to turn on the lights. He wanted to see every inch of her.

Together, they quickly took care of the curtains, and Presley retrieved two condoms from his case before flicking on the small light that sat over the bed for reading. Taking Nova's hand, he tugged her to stand in front of him. "We know everything about each other, except this. You're going to have to tell me how you like it, Nova. And I'll do the same, yeah?"

She placed her hands on his ribs, running them over the ridges of his abs. He wasn't a guy known for being shy about his body, but he was relieved he was in the best shape of his life for this.

"I'm nervous, Presley."

He placed his hands over hers. "You know what, Nov. I am too. Yes, I want this, I want you. But more than that, I want this to be special. I think our first time should be important."

She nodded.

"If you aren't ready, I can go get the fire started, we can pull on comfy clothes, and we can go snuggle up on the sofa. I'll even watch the second *Nativity* movie. There isn't a time limit on this."

"And that right there is the reason I'm ready."

"You are?"

Nova nodded. "Kiss me, Presley."

He did as she asked, cupping her cheek, and slipping into the sweet taste of her. Sugar and champagne. Her lips softened against his as her hands slid around his waist. Skin against skin, he groaned. There wasn't a better feeling in the world than Nova's body lined up against him. Even as he had to bend to reach her. Bending further, he gripped her thighs and hoisted her into his arms as her legs wrapped around him. Placing a knee on the bed, he lowered her to the cool cotton.

The boat should feel cold with no heat or fire, but their bodies were hot for each other. The long column of her neck, so pale compared to his warm California tan, was soft beneath his lips as her fingertips dragged over his skin.

He trailed kisses over her shoulder to her breasts, scooping one into his hand and drawing the nipple into his mouth.

Nova arched beneath him, and suddenly he wanted to know every single piece of her intimately. As he kissed his way lower, her fingers threaded their way into his hair. "Presley," she gasped, as his tongue touched her clit for the very first time, lighting a match to his powder keg of need.

10

NOVA

Worries about the reality of this being her and Presley fled. Two decades of friendship were replaced with an insatiable need for what he was offering.

He was a puppeteer, making her body move and feel things she didn't know were possible. As his tongue sought her, delving within in her then returning to circle her clit, she got lost in the sensations of it all.

Nova wove her fingers deeper through Presley's dark hair and bent her knees, urging him deeper, grinding against him harder.

"There," she gasped when he hit the place guaranteed to make her come.

Her legs began to shake as her orgasm began to build.

"You like that, Nov?" he said, his voice ripe with a need she felt down to her bones.

"Mm-hm," she moaned, the intensity building. "Presley."

He added a finger, then another, as he sucked her clit into his mouth. The move detonated an orgasm so bold and beautiful it slammed into her, sending sparks of light to her peripheral vision. She flopped her head back as wave after wave of pleasure overtook her.

Maybe she gasped. Maybe she moaned. She couldn't remember as Presley eased his actions and climbed up her body to kiss her soundly, the taste of her on his lips.

"You taste so good," he muttered against her lips.

"And I want to taste you," she replied. She let her hand slip down to his cock, squeezing it from root to tip.

Presley's eyes rolled back, and he groaned before swiftly pulling away from her to reach for the condom. "As incredible as that sounds, I'm going to need to take a rain check on that, because there's only one place I want my dick right now, and that's deep inside you."

In the soft light, she watched as he rolled the condom on. His cock was wide and long, unsurprising given the size of the rest of him. He was also quite possibly the largest guy she'd ever been with, and she couldn't wait to learn how it would feel.

"Ready?" Presley asked as he climbed over her.

"Very."

His eyes held hers as he lined the tip up with her entrance and stroked her. A gentle back-and-forth over her tender clit, bathing in her wetness, before easing inside her, one inch at a time.

"Nov," he groaned. "Fuck, that feels good." With each stroke, he slid further into her, a delicious stretch and burn followed by heat and ease.

His lips met hers as he lost patience, thrusting more deeply until he was fully seated in her.

Her breath came in short bursts. Pinned beneath his large frame, there was nothing else she could do. But she didn't want him to move. She needed this. To have all choices for movement taken away, to be left with what he wanted and how he wanted them.

While their kiss lost all semblance of control, his hands still cupped her cheeks gently.

She ran her palms over his shoulders, down the muscles of his back, to the dip of his butt which was as firm as she'd imagined it would be. Every part of him felt as foreign as it felt familiar as she got to know him in the intimate way she'd only dreamed of.

She eased her knees up and Presley groaned. "Just like that, Nov."

He slid his hands beneath her, holding her where he wanted her, but she sensed he was holding back. She placed her palm to his cheek. "Take me, Presley."

"Yeah?"

She nodded. "Yeah."

His moves became more frenetic, his hips thrusting into her over and over, her hips rising to meet him every time. Sweat gathered between their bodies. Their lips met, a passionate coming together, his tongue duelling with hers. His hands swept over her body, exploring every inch of her, setting her skin on fire.

Sex had never felt so utterly consuming, so deeply satisfying, so filled with promise.

The realisation she was on the path to orgasm hit her by surprise. "I don't usually come twice," she said, embarrassed when she realised she'd said it out loud.

"Well, there's a challenge if . . . ever I heard . . . one," Presley grunted.

He shifted his position slightly so he slid more directly against her clit, and within three seconds, she fell apart beneath him. "Presley," she groaned.

"You feel so good squeezing me like that. Shit. I'm gonna come, babe."

Holding her tight, he pulsed deep inside her. He'd thrown his head back. She couldn't see his eyes, but delicious contortions of pleasure corded the muscles of his neck.

When he flopped down over her, still buried in her, she ran her fingers over his back, into his hair. She squeezed his neck, touching him everywhere.

Their world had just changed in the most epic of ways, but outside the boat, the world was exactly the same. The juxtaposition as exciting as it was terrifying.

But something that felt so good couldn't be wrong. Right?

"I'll move in a second," Presley said, his voice muffled against the pillow. He turned and kissed the side of her neck, the move tickling.

She wiggled beneath him as she laughed.

"God, your laugh is enough to get me hard all over again. It's catnip to my dick."

He reached between them and slid out of her, before disappearing into the bathroom for a moment. When he returned, there was a smile on his face she hadn't seen since they were younger. It was a shy smile. And the thought she'd reduced him to the less confident young man he used to be, rather than the confident Hollywood A-lister he was now, warmed something inside her.

When he appeared on the big screen, he seemed larger than life. So commanding, the hero of the hour, the capable and courageous love interest. Now, he was just Presley.

Taking her hand, he tugged her from the bed, catching her against his body for a hug before pulling back the covers and encouraging her to slide beneath them. Within a minute, they were curled up against each other in a cotton cocoon.

"Can I tell you something?" he asked, his face so close to hers theirs noses touched.

"What's that?"

"I've imagined what it would be like. You and me. But it was a million times better. And I really hope you feel the same way about it, because I'd really like to do that again."

She touched her fingertips to his cheek and kissed him sweetly. "I feel the same way. And I'd really like to do it again. But perhaps in the morning. You can be my Christmas present."

"And you can be mine."

They lay there, side by side, in silence. Their fingers and bodies saying everything that needed to be said. Heartfelt kisses, touches filled with longing. A quiet exploration, until Minerva pounced on the bed.

"Unf," Presley groaned, taking the brunt of her leap. "I thought you said she liked me."

Nova laughed. "She's just trying to grab our fingers moving beneath the blanket."

"I'm going to move her to the living room and close the door to the bathroom so she can't get to us."

"She'll just miaow until you open it again. Plus, I think she wants to settle on your chest again like she did the other night."

Presley nudged Minerva out of the way and tugged Nova closer. She rested her head on his chest as his arm slipped around her, his fingers resting on her bicep. "I'd rather have you sleeping on my chest," he said.

She played with the sprinkling of chest hair that she

assumed was manscaped into submission, given the perfect symmetry of it. Here, in the safety of his arms on the boat, it was easy to forget they weren't simply two people dangling over the precipice of love. Worries about how their relationship would work in practice needed to be banked and saved until another day.

"When are you supposed to leave?" she asked.

Presley yawned and reached up to click the light off, casting them into darkness. "Not until the third. We still have at least a week."

"Hmm."

"We'll figure it out, Nov. You and me. How it works. We've managed to keep our friendship alive this long. We'll figure out how to keep this version of our relationship alive too."

"I'm going to hold you to that."

His arms tightened around her, and she stroked Minerva, who'd settled herself on Presley's stomach. "Promise me you won't bitch when I pay for all your travel, and we'll be fine."

"Only if you promise to fly me economy."

She felt his chest shake with soft laughter. "I was going to send a jet, so we can compromise on business class, and you can just deal with it."

"Bossy."

Presley kissed the top of her head. "Maybe. But do we have a deal?"

"We do."

"Good. Oh, and if I feel like getting handsy when you're half-awake in the morning, do I have your consent to wake you with any part of my anatomy that feels like it?"

Now it was her turn to chuckle as she rolled over in his arms so he could spoon her close. "Most definitely. I look forward to being surprised by whichever part of your anatomy steps up to bat."

He kissed the side of her neck. "Now go to sleep, babe."

And she did as he said, drifting off into the deepest of sleeps.

11

PRESLEY

Presley silently lifted the covers of the bed and climbed out. He'd said he was going to wake her with a part of his body, and certainly his dick had risen to the challenge already. In the past relationships he'd had, his actions had been governed by his sexual urges. Hell, it was the reason he was on Nova's boat. But something about Nova made him want it all. The sex and the softness. The intensity and need along with the emotion and care.

In the dark, he made his way through the bathroom to his case, and, using the flashlight on his phone, he grabbed some joggers and a hoodie. Minerva wrapped her way around his feet, a trip hazard if ever there was one. The boat was fucking cold, and he shivered as he dressed.

Ever thankful for Nova's diligent boat maintenance—she'd left the fire built and ready to light—he took just a moment or two to strike a match and send the paper and kindling to burn. The crackle and hiss of the fire starting plus the romance of the flames stuttering to life made everything feel cosy, as if he lived in a snow globe.

The world outside was silent. No whisper of wind, no

roar of traffic or chatter of people that plagued him in LA. Just the peace of Christmas morning on the canal. Once the basic necessity of fire was taken care of, he debated turning on the engine so he could heat the radiators too, but he didn't want Nova to wake yet. Nor did he want to break the silence.

As quietly as possible, he made his way to the kitchen and put the light on. As he filled the kettle, he caught sight of his reflection in the window overlooking the canal and tall natural stone on the opposite bank. His hair stood up in every direction, but he was smiling and hadn't even realised it.

Last night had been everything he'd hoped for and more. And if he was really lucky, he could do it all over again today. Sure, his career was still up the shitter, and who knew what else was being said about him in the outside world, but right now, he was happy.

"Merry Christmas," he whispered to himself. Once the kettle was full and heating, he texted a quick message to his mum, wishing her a Merry Christmas and telling her about their last-minute decision to move the boat to Llangollen and that it had been fun to steer it.

It was nearly seven a.m., but it was still dark outside, partly because of the time of year, but also because of the sheltered nature of their position.

His phone vibrated with a reply from his mum.

Merry Christmas, Presley. You always loved that truck game in the arcade, the one with the big horn on it. Not surprised you like driving the boat. Hope I get to see you before you go back. Love, Mum. p.s. I saw the headlines about the other stuff. Do I need to worry about you?

It was a fair question. He texted quickly. *Stupid mistake and lesson learned. Glad I'm able to hide out here with Nova.*

Dots appeared, then the response from his mum. *Well, thank her from me and pass along a hug.*

Doing that would be a pleasure. Perhaps he'd pass along a kiss too.

He responded that he'd try to make a stop at hers but that she was welcome to come out and see him in California to escape dreary January rain.

The kettle began to whistle, and he was able to turn off the heat it before it reached its crescendo. Once the two cups of tea were made, he wandered back to the bedroom, shivering with cold. While the fire heated the living area quickly, it took a while for the warmth to find its way through the entire boat.

He placed the cups on the small shelf on the other side of the boat from the bed, slipped off his clothes, then climbed back under the blankets.

Warmth enveloped him immediately.

"Ahh," Nova said, her body flinching away from him. "You're cold."

"If you'd stop wiggling I'd be warm again," he said, reaching around her tugging her closer.

"It's not fair that you can overpower me," she muttered, rolling over in his arms and offering her face up for a kiss.

Which of course he indulged.

"You liked it when I overpowered you last night."

"That is the embarrassing truth of it."

Presley grinned. "All's fair in love and sex, babe." Playfully, he nuzzled the side of her neck. "I made tea."

"Oh, God. You might just be the perfect boyfriend."

The word boyfriend shocked him for a moment. Is that what they were now? It seemed a quick assumption of the mantle, but despite the initial shock of hearing her say it, he realised he liked it. He liked the idea of being Nova's.

"I was cold, and you didn't want to warm me up. Does that make you the worst girlfriend?"

"It's quite possible I'm getting the better end of this deal."

"Just remember that." He sat up and reached over to grab the tea and pass a cup to her. "Does this make us officially old—sitting on a canal boat under the blankets sipping tea instead of making out on luxurious Egyptian cotton in a five-star hotel in Bora Bora?"

"Meh. I think both things sound great. Can I ask you something?"

He pulled the blankets further up his chest, waiting for the heat from the fire to start to fill the boat. "Anything, what's up?"

"I don't need a big discussion about this, but you and those two women. Is that something you like? Two women at once? Because I can't be that woman for you. I'd be too jealous."

Christ, how many ways was that decision going to trip him up? "No. I mean, sure, it's always fun to try something different. It was the first time I'd done it. It wasn't even intentional. But even if this wasn't happening between the two of us, I wouldn't be doing it again." He reached for the hand not holding the tea and squeezed it. "Too many arms and legs, not enough bed space, and I couldn't concentrate. Found it stressful trying to be . . . well, fair, if you know what I mean."

Nova chuckled softly. "Okay. I just . . . well, I woke up at three o'clock this morning with my mind on a rollercoaster about it. And were you safe?"

"To be honest, I think so, but I can't be certain. There was . . . evidence I'd been safe. But I got tested two days later when I realised I'd been stupid. Everything came back fine, and I haven't been with anyone else recently."

"Okay." Nova looked down at her cup.

"Hey, what else is on your mind?"

She shook her head. "I'm just being stupid and feeling a bit awkward. I don't know. I guess I always wanted to just be Nova in your eyes. The girl who was lucky enough to have you as a best friend. Where I could be a bit weird, and you wouldn't judge. And now, you're naked, in my bed, drinking tea, and while last night was amazing, it's now morning, and I'm not sure what I'm supposed to say to you. And how am I supposed to get up and pretend like nothing happened? Or is that the point? I'm supposed to wake up and pretend everything happened and figure out how to be some kind of sex siren you'll fall in love with. And why the heck am I talking about love because that's . . . see . . . I'm off the rails and I'm rambling . . . Jesus. I need to shut up."

Presley laughed, took the cup from her hand, and placed both mugs on the floor. "Come here." He tugged her until she was sitting astraddle his hips with the duvet pulled up over her shoulders. Her hair was wild, and he knew she'd be mad she hadn't braided it before they went to bed, but her eyes were bright and clear.

And her tits looked delicious as she placed her palms on his chest, but he'd save telling her that until later. "Nova. It's just you and me. And I already love that you ramble when you're nervous. Or that you go super quiet when you are borderline terrified. And I don't expect you to turn into anybody you aren't. Because I have always loved who you are. And as for the sex siren thing? I don't know how to explain this without making you a little bit mad, but I jerked off after we had that hour long video conversation about how you were going to insulate the boat. If you recall, you were wearing a boiler suit and had your hair in a head scarf and hadn't showered for three days because the hot water wasn't working in the boat. I convinced myself it was nothing to do with you and all about being tired and bored, but really, it was about watching your lips as you talk and a burning urge to lower the zipper of the boiler suit. But the point of that is: I don't want you to be anyone other than you. You turn me on and make me laugh and see the side of me that nobody else does, just by being you."

His hands caged her ribs, and his thumbs brushed the underside of her breasts then stroked her nipples.

"Sweet talker," she said, but the last syllable hitched.

Looking up at her face, he pinched the erect buds. Watching her eyes go wide and her hips roll over his dick involuntarily had him hard all over again. "You know how much fun it's going to be getting to know your body?"

"Tell me more," she said.

"Really?"

"Yeah. I want to hear it."

Presley wiggled down the bed a little, lifting her hips a fraction then settling her directly over his dick. "That's better," he said. "You know how hot your pussy looks right now?" How did he not know she kept it bare? If he'd had to guess, he would have said full bush, not that he cared either way.

Nova bit down on her lip and lowered her eyes. As if she liked the compliment but was also embarrassed by it as the same time.

"Okay. So, here's what I'm thinking. There's the obvious. I can't wait to learn all the weird things that turn you on."

"Weird things?" Nova sat up, lifting her palms off his chest, back arched.

Unable to resist, he cupped her breasts, squeezing them

firmly. The reaction was the same as it was to her nipples. And he realised he had himself a woman with the kind of sensitive breasts linked directly to her clit by some kind of sexual superhighway.

"We all know the obvious, right? Playing with the good bits." He tugged on her nipples again garnering another gasp. "It's fucking hot that you like that, Nov. But it's the out of the ordinary. The back of the knee." He ran his hands down her ribs and then pressed his thumb into the crease of her hip, making her jump. "Here." He reached for her arm and pulled her close to lick the crease of her elbow. "Here maybe." He tugged her forward so that she fell onto him and then fisted a handful of her hair. Tilting her neck, he breathed softly against her ear before biting on the lobe. "Here."

"Those feel like good bits too," Nova gasped.

"Yeah? What about here?" He nibbled his way along her collar bone as he felt her wetness begin to coat his dick. She began to sway back and forth over him, her lips dragging along his length.

It would take nothing to slide into her. "Babe?"

"Yes," she whispered.

"Condoms? I've been tested, I promise. Do I need to put one on or can I just go with this?" He rolled his hips one last time knowing he shouldn't do it again given he was certain his dick had already begun to leak.

Nova didn't answer. Just reached between them and angled him before sitting back on him.

"Fuck," both gasped at the exact same time. It made Nova giggle, and he couldn't help but grin.

She rose up and then sank back down over him, just as he lifted his hips to meet her. Quickly easing into her was a sign that she'd adjust to his width. God, he couldn't remember ever not using a condom. The feel of skin on skin. To feel her warmth, how wet she was for him, launched everything to such a level of sensitivity, he wasn't sure he'd last.

"Sit up, Nov. Let me watch."

Nova did as he said, setting a slow and decidedly painful pace. "Tell me more. About what you want to do to me."

Dirty talk he was down with. "I want to learn all the sexual things you enjoy, things you want to try. I want you to suck me off in front of the fire, and I'd really like to fuck your tits at some point while I tug on your nipples."

Nova lost her rhythm for a moment, then regained her focus. "That sounds . . . hot."

"It will be."

"I meant sitting in front of the fire."

He looked up at her, away from the sight of his dick sliding deep inside of her and the sight of her creamy arousal as he withdrew. "Funny girl. I want to fuck you from behind because you've always had a fit ass." He reached behind her and squeezed her butt, changing the action of her hips until she was riding him like a rodeo bull. More of a grind and slip than rise and pull.

"Ass? How American," she gasped as he realised he was going to come.

Soon.

He slipped his thumb to her clit, circling it, and reached his other hand to her breast, teasing her nipple. Squeezing it, tugging it, twisting it, until Nova slammed her hands to his chest and shuddered through her orgasm. Every part of her clenched at him. And every part of him responded. His chest ached with the want of her, his body surged for completion, but his heart burst in the most glorious of ways when she flipped her hair over her shoulder and smiled at him.

And as he came, he realised if she ever asked him again what he wanted to do to her, his answer would be to always makes her smile.

12

NOVA

As Nova vacuumed the floor of the bedroom, she wondered what day it was.

Was it Tuesday? Or Wednesday? She couldn't remember how many days had passed since Christmas, and the fact she couldn't was just about the only thing Presley was right about with his assessment of the holiday. Time ebbed and flowed, so filled with brie and red wine and movies and After Eight Mints and Twiglets and great sex, that she wasn't sure which way was up.

Today, she'd woken up before him, so she'd crept out of bed and finished her morning boat routine before Presley had ambled to the kitchen in just a pair of low-hung joggers that revealed the delicious lines of his body. They'd sipped coffee and braved opening the side hatch to throw bread to the swans.

After a handful of days of pure indulgence and more sex than she'd had in the last year combined, more mundane tasks required attention. Laundry needed to be done. The fireplace needed a proper cleaning. And the boat needed some thorough housekeeping.

They'd amiably shared the chores, and when Presley mentioned needing to go for a run, she'd suggested he go now before the rain started, while she finished the vacuuming.

She put the vacuum cleaner away in the entrance cupboard, then placed the kettle on the gas burner to boil water for tea. A client had sent her a new manuscript early. A women's fiction story about a hedonistic female singer during the halcyon days of Studio 54. It was set in the seventies, and Nova couldn't wait to take a peek.

Work hadn't been in the front of her mind for days. Her schedule hadn't required her to start back until the second of January. But perhaps she could get ahead.

Once she'd made her tea, she gathered her laptop and set up at the dinette. With her first sip, she dove into the manuscript.

They say you could find the shadow of yourself at Studio 54. In its dimly lit corners and rooms, with a soundtrack of disco and strangers fucking, it was possible to become, for a moment, the most dangerous version of you.

The hedonist.

The addict.

The whore.

Surrounded by people infinitely more attractive, more exciting, more rapacious, it was impossible to not look inwards and conclude you were infinitely lacking.

And for the first time in my life, I felt the lack to the deepest marrow of my bones.

Urgh . . . she wished she could write like that. A mood set in less than ninety words.

She glanced to her poetry book, tucked up on the shelf.

Maybe she did in her own way.

Perhaps she needed to get another opinion, to pull the

best from her poems and build a themed compilation. When Presley went back home, it would give her something to do in the evenings. It was strange that so much of her time had been spent alone on the boat, never lonely, but she knew Presley's departure was going to leave a massive hole.

She was just about to read on when the first heavy splat of rain hit the side hatch window. It was quickly followed by another. And another, and suddenly a total deluge bounced off the canal and the roof of the boat.

The sound of rain had always soothed her. She figured it was because her parents had often planned their travel around the sunniest of climates. To her, the scent of fresh cut grass and the sound of raindrops always signified a return home.

Cupping her tea, she watched as a family of ducks hurried for the bank opposite.

Within minutes, the door to the rear of the boat burst open, and a sodden Presley stepped down the wooden stairs. "Fuck me."

"Don't move," she shouted through laughter, hurrying to the bathroom to get him a towel. "You'll get water everywhere."

He shook his head anyway, brushing his hair back from his face. "That came out of nowhere."

When she handed him the towel, he used it to tug her towards him. "Ah. Don't get me wet," she said as she tried to push against his chest.

He pressed his lips to hers and cupped her cheek with a cold hand. "But I like getting you wet."

"You're all soggy."

He stepped back and yanked his soaked hoodie and T-shirt over his head, letting it plop to the floor. "Better," he said before kissing her again. "Because I have a whole lot of energy and nowhere to put it."

"You're cold," she said, trying to wriggle out of his grasp, but he slid his hands beneath her sweater and lifted it above her bra.

"Pretty," he said, running a finger over the lace. "Help me get warm, babe. I don't want to get sick."

Nova rolled her eyes. "Get sick, my ass."

"Ass? How American," he said, repeating her earlier words back to her.

But she let him manhandle her anyway, because it was Presley, and his dimples were prominent in his flushed cheeks.

He kicked off his trainers and tugged off his shorts.

"The curtains are open," she breathed against his lips.

"I don't give a fuck. And no one is out there." He lifted her onto the counter, tugged her slippers off her feet, pushed her skirt up her thighs, and wiggled her panties down her legs.

"We just cleaned the counter."

"I'll clean it again. Perfect fucking pussy." He tugged her to the edge of the counter before burying his face between her legs to circle her clit with his tongue.

She raised one foot to the edge of the counter and groaned.

Presley stood and palmed his cock, already hard. "You look so fucking hot like that. Tousled. Pretty pink bra. Legs wide open for me."

She reached for his hard length, and he let her take it, almost pulling him to where she needed him. "Less talking, more fucking."

The smile on his face made her grin.

"Your wish, my command." He lined himself up with her

opening and thrust into her, seating himself halfway before withdrawing and pushing himself home. "God, Nov. How do you always feel so good?"

She wrapped her arms around him and placed her lips to his ear. "You make me this wet."

"Fuck," he groaned, beginning to thrust.

"Jesus. It's raining harder than a . . . oh dear God. Sorry. I'll just . . . be outside." The clatter of the boat doors told her that their guest with the familiar voice was gone.

"Fuck," Presley muttered as he pulled out of her and reached for the towel they abandoned, wrapping it around his waist.

Nova looked down at the obvious erection. "I don't think that's going to make your mum more comfortable."

Presley looked up at the ceiling. "It was the best of times, it was the worst of times, it was the age of wisdom, it was the age of foolishness, it was the epoch of disbelief, it was the epoch of incredulity."

"Dickens?" she hissed as she pulled her sweater over her head.

Presley opened one eye and looked at her. "Only thing guaranteed to kill this boner. My balls are going to explode. *It was the season of light. It was the season of darkness. It was the spring of hope.* Shit, it's not working."

She opened the small narrow window. "It smells of sex in here. Go to the bedroom and take a minute. Or three if you need. There are tissues by the bed. I'll . . . make tea or something."

He tossed all his wet clothes into the kitchen sink, and she waited until he'd disappeared through the bathroom before she patted down her hair, sweater, and skirt. As she was about to open the door, she saw her panties in a wet heap. Quickly, she buried them beneath Presley's wet clothes, and opened the door where Sally blew warmth into her hands on the tented stern.

"I'm so sorry, Sally. I didn't know you were coming. Quick, come inside."

"Hey, Nova, sweetheart. I'm sorry I . . . well, I should have knocked. It was just raining so hard, and I was cold and wanted to surprise you."

Nova winded. "I'm sorry. Let's get you warm and then we can catch you up."

Sally followed her down the stairs and by the time the simplest formalities had been met—coat hung, a place to put her purse, shoes removed—Presley appeared from the bedroom.

"Mum," he said, obviously pleased to see her, but hopefully as embarrassed as Nova felt. Sally hugged him and he led her to the sofa while Nova put the kettle on.

"I was headed home, and when I checked the map, it was only forty minutes out of my way to stop by."

There was an awkward pause and Nova busied herself with the tea.

"So, you and Nova?" Sally asked.

As Nova carried the cups to the living room, Presley looked up at her. "Yeah. Me and Nova."

Sally clapped her hands and took the cup Nova offered. "Excellent. I mean, I didn't need to see proof, but I'm glad it's you, Nova. You've been a part of our family for so long it makes sense. But . . . how?"

"You said you didn't need proof, Mum."

Sally grimaced. "Not that kind of information. But, when did this happen?"

When she sat down next to Presley, he took her hand. "Technically, four days ago. In reality, it's been on my mind for a while. It took screwing up and Nova being there for me to realise just what we had."

"And are you okay with what happened, Nova?"

She could see the genuine concern in Sally's eyes. "It's not something I really want to think about in great detail. But it happened before the two of us, well . . . you know. If they'd not taken photographs, I'd find it easier to move on from. But they've done damage to get their fifteen minutes of fame. Damage that needs repairing, and that's wrong."

"Well," Sally said, patting Nova's knee. "Not that I had any doubt of what your stance would be, I'm pleased to hear you have Presley's back."

Nova took a breath. "I'm sure there'll be some more fallout when Presley re-emerges though. Right?"

Presley shrugged. "Probably. But Narmin and the team are putting together a plan for me when I head back to LA."

"And when is that?" Sally asked.

"The third."

"Is Nova going with you? It might look better if you have a girlfriend by your side."

Presley looked over at her. "We're still ironing out the details."

Nova bit her lip, she hadn't told this to Presley, but she was certain of it. "I don't think it's a good idea for me to suddenly appear by his side."

"You don't?" Presley asked. She could hear the concern and unspoken question in his tone.

She shook her head. "I don't. It's too convenient. And people won't believe it because I've been in the press with you before. They know we're friends. We're not a secret. It's too close to what happened too. And if we lied to say we were in a relationship, then I look like a sucker. I just think it's better to keep this private for a while. Until it all blows over."

Presley's shoulders sagged with relief. "I thought you were saying something else then."

That she was having second thoughts about the two of them.

She ran her fingers through his drying hair. "Not at all. Plus, I prefer this. Just you and me. I prefer this version of you to the Hollywood one."

13

PRESLEY

"The Savoy?" Nova said, stating the obvious two days later, as she looked up at the giant letters above the small water fountain their limo circled. She placed her nose to the glass, like a child at the sweet shop window. "You brought us to London to stay at The Savoy?"

Presley grinned. "I did. I thought we could have some fun. Stay here tonight and for New Year's Eve tomorrow. Then head back to the boat."

"Ahh," she said, flinging herself across his lap to hug him. "You are the best."

She looked every inch the rock star, like she'd just fallen straight off the screen in *Almost Famous*. Black fitted jeans that kicked out in flared at the bottom, a white blouse that made him think of early Stevie Nicks, and a long flowing top—part cardigan, part kaftan, part scarf . . . he still wasn't sure how the thing worked—in swirls of black and muddy orange.

If they were lucky, everyone would look at her and

nobody would notice who he was, and they could float through their time here.

"And you were so grumpy when I told you I was taking you somewhere this morning," he said, holding her close.

"In fairness, you woke me up at six a.m. and told me I had ninety minutes to pack and shower."

"In *fairness*, I made you a cup of tea and thought ninety minutes would be plenty of time."

Nova laughed. "You used up fifteen trying to have sex with me in the tiny shower. I tried to tell you we wouldn't fit."

He kissed the side of her neck as the driver stepped out of the limo. "Yes, but it was all kinds of slippery fun trying." Until he'd given up, bent her over the sink and fucked her.

When they entered their suite after a few moments at reception, Nova ran around, oohing and ahhing over everything in sight. He quickly checked his phone, ignoring the fabulous view of the river and the London Eye.

I don't know what you're playing at but stop avoiding me and pick up the phone.

His stomach tightened. He *was* avoiding his agent. He was avoiding the whole goddamn mess.

Unless it's a chance to speak with Harriet directly, could you leave me alone until the New Year, please? I can't deal. He knew he was burying his head in the sand, but the thought of having to rebuild everything he knew was too big.

Unexpectedly, the little dots bounced, telling him Narmin was replying. It was five in the morning in LA, but then again, Narmin rarely slept.

We're on the same side. I'm working on something. It can wait until the first but no longer.

Thanks, Narmin.

Yeah, just keep your head down.

He shouldn't have brought Nova to London, he knew it. He should have booked them somewhere small, private. Taken her to Scotland or something. But he knew the small-town girl from Devon secretly loved the Big Smoke. And all the Christmas lights would still be up in store fronts.

"There's plenty of room for two in this shower," Nova yelled from the bathroom. "And the tub could sleep a family of four."

"We'll try that later," he shouted in reply. "Want to go walking?"

Her face popped back around the door frame. "Yes. All the yeses in the world, yes."

He checked his outfit in the mirror. Instead of the cool leather jacket he'd arrived with, he wore the waterproof fleece and coat from the boat. With a thick hat on his head, a warm scarf wrapped around his neck, and dark sunglasses on, he could have been anybody.

They set out, decided to meander, and then Nova led them toward Carnaby Street without so much as a glance anywhere else, like he knew she would.

As they approached the start of Carnaby Street, Nova grabbed his arm. "Oh my gosh, do you remember that steak house we went to that time? Where they had those Argentinian prawns with that chilli and shiso leaf dressing that was just to die for."

"I do," he said casually. Glad she'd remembered. "Are you hungry, before we start shopping? We ate breakfast nearly seven hours ago."

Nova nodded. "Especially now I remembered those prawns. Can we find somewhere we can get seafood?"

He took her hand and led her west a couple of streets and—

"Oh my God. This is it. I hadn't realised we were so close."

Presley grinned and opened the door. "The prawns are yours. Have them for starter and entrée. Even dessert if you like."

The maître d' met them and, seeing his face, nodded. "Welcome, sir. Your room is this way."

Nova looked at him. "Your room?" she mouthed.

Presley winked. She didn't have to know the extra he'd paid so they could sit in a private room and order from the evening à la carte menu rather than the lunch menu, just so she could get the prawns.

Once they were seated with wine, in the private dining that sat ten but only held the two of them, Nova pointed her glass in his direction. "Your cunning knows no bounds, Mr. James. You remembered I love this place."

"You remember the promise you made with me this morning?"

"Which one? The one where I promised I would get you back for turning the shower to cold? Or the promise to burn all your underwear if you kept putting your cold hands beneath my jumper in the limo?"

Presley sipped the pinot noir from Sonoma County that cost ten times what the Tesco wine had cost. While he noticed the difference, he doubted Nova cared one way or the other. "No, the promise where I said that no matter what, you had to let me pay for this trip to repay you for helping me lay low."

She leaned forward, across the table, and reached for his hand. "I told you then, and I'll repeat myself now, you don't owe me for that. I'm just happy to see you. The banging is a bonus."

Presley spluttered as he sipped and then put the glass down. "My dick is just a bonus."

Nova placed her glass to her lips and smiled before taking a sip. "I mean, it's a pretty epic bonus, but still."

He shook his head. "I don't think my sexual prowess has ever been called a bonus. But just let me pay. For whatever I want to, Nova. Yes?"

"Fine. Because you asked nicely. And because you arranged this and remembered I loved it so much the last time we were here."

"Good. And while we're at it, I want to talk logistics. I meant what I said, Nov. I don't want to be away from you unless I need to. I see why you love the boat, and I'm not asking you to sell it and move. But my work isn't as flexible location-wise, and your work is mobile with more flexibility than I have. Can we agree that you'll come out to see me, wherever I am, at least once a month for a week or whatever, and whenever I'm not filming, I do the same, so we see each other at least half the month while I'm not filming? And then, when I'm filming, we'll play it by ear?"

Just as Nova opened her mouth the answer, there was a knock on the door and their food was brought inside. Gluttonously, Nova had asked for it to come all at once. She'd argued their starters of the prawns—two servings—and the lobster plus their steaks made a surf and turf.

"Oh my God," Nova moaned as she stuffed a prawn into her mouth. "They are just as good as I remember."

At least, that's what he thought she'd said through the mouthful of food. They ate for a few moments in silence, trying bits of food off each other's plates. When she paused to take a drink, he reached for her hand.

"Nov. I need to know we're going to see each other."

"Yes, I'll come. I'll book the boat into a marina once a

month. It'll take a little bit of planning, might be three weeks, might be five depending on the canal."

A band that he hadn't realised was squeezing his chest released. "Good. Because, honestly, there's no point having all that money if it means I don't get to see you. And my schedule won't be like this forever. Hell, it might not even be that busy next year given what I've been laying low from. But I don't want a single pound of it if I don't have you to share it with."

Nova tipped her head to the side, the weak winter sunlight catching her hair, setting it on fire. "That might be the sweetest thing you've ever said to me."

Sometimes, when she looked at him like that, her eyes so clear, a soft smile on her lips, her cheeks flushed, he could barely catch his breath. "You'd be surprised at what I'm capable of when it comes to you."

When they finished dinner, he followed her around the huge Liberty store in Mayfair as she touched eighty percent of the things she walked by, commenting on textures and scents and patterns. He was more taken by the interior which always reminded him of a glass roofed playhouse of Elizabethan players. In MAC, they'd argued, and then she'd given in to him buying her a dozen different things she'd lovingly caressed and studied. Palettes, lipsticks, mascaras, and other shit he didn't really care about because he was too busy watching her.

She'd threatened to go home on the train if he didn't let her buy him a pair of Old Skools at the Vans store on Carnaby Street, so he had. They stayed until it went dark so they could get the full effect of all the store windows on the way home.

As they walked back to the hotel with all their bags, she spotted a bookstore.

"One more stop," she said. "I promise it will be the last."

"It's not a chore, shopping with you," he said, squeezing her mittened hand. "We've always done normal stuff together. Just because we do other things now too doesn't mean we can't still do this."

Nova laughed. "I feel like *other things* should be in quotes with a wink."

He held the door open to the bookstore. "I saw your writing," he said. "I didn't know you still did it."

"Oh, it's a hobby," she said, brushing the comment away with her hand as she studied the store map.

"It was beautiful. What you wrote. I didn't flick through your book or anything, but the poem that was open was so expressive. It told a whole love story so succinctly."

When she turned to face him, he was surprised by the uncertainty. "You thought so."

"I know so. You need to publish your writing."

She sighed and led him up the escalator. "There are millions of people around the world scribbling their thoughts and musings into little notebooks. Doesn't mean they should all be published."

When they got to the top, he tugged her to a stop. "But yours should."

Nova looked away from him, at the racks of books, the ceiling, the floor, then her eyes met his. "You want to see some more?"

"I do."

"Then maybe I'll show you," she said. "But we're here to look at the words other people have put out into the world. *Their* truths."

And one day, the world was going to see hers.

He'd make sure of it.

14

NOVA

"You need to stop now," Nova said the following evening as she sipped champagne and viewed the room through the exquisite eye mask that had been delivered to their room that morning. "The trip. The hotel. The limo. The spending spree. This . . ."

From their table on the balcony where they'd just eaten a delicious five-course meal served up by a Michelin star chef, she looked out over the luxury of the private member's club masquerade ball to celebrate New Year's Eve. People danced without inhibition, and she was certain that despite the masks, she'd identified at least two other Hollywood A-listers and a disgraced dictator.

When Presley's dimples showed, she knew he wasn't even sorry. "I'll stop when I'm ready."

"Okay. Tell me this doesn't have an *Eyes Wide Shut* vibe though. Like how do I know there isn't some ritualistic fucking going on somewhere in a cavern below the dance floor? I'm not going down any dark corridors with strangers, no matter how hot they look in a cape."

"You edit too many fantasy books, babe. Anyway, the only person I want to fuck in a cavern below the dance floor is you, with or without a cape. Plus, this was the only way we could go out tonight with any hope of remaining anonymous. This club has venues around the world, the price tag makes it exclusive. There are privacy rules everyone respects, or their membership is revoked. And the mask gives us an added anonymity, which—looking at you in that dress—is so hot."

She looked down at the tightly fitted black gothic gown with panels of lace, see-through in places, that had arrived with the masks. "As gorgeous as this is, it's another example of you needing to stop."

He smirked as he sipped more of his champagne. "Not until we are back on the boat tomorrow. Like Cinderella's midnight curfew, all of this ends when you place your key in the lock of the boat."

"Hmm. Cinderella, huh? Does this make you my Prince Charming?"

"I think only you can answer that one." He raised an eyebrow, waiting for a response.

She shrugged. "Meh. You'll do."

Presley laughed, his dimples popping. "I guess I'll be spending next year trying to prove to you that I am."

"Fine. You already are. What other New Year's resolutions do you have?"

"My main one is to make this movie. I think it'll crush me for a long time if Hattie Lee passes this role onto someone else. So, my main goal is to land that role."

"And what else. Personally?"

"Beyond making out with you every chance I get?"

She threw her napkin at him. "That's not a valid New Year's resolution."

"Okay. Persuading you to fall irrevocably in love with me. Does that count?"

Nova smiled despite herself. "Yes. You can include that one. It should take until at least June. What else?"

Presley shrugged. "I haven't really thought beyond that. I have a job. I stay in shape for a job. I manage the finances from that job. That's been my life. And I'm not mad about it. It's served me well."

"But don't you want more?"

He reached for the leg of her chair and tugged her a little closer. "You were too far away," he whispered against her ear.

"Sweet talker. But more? Have you thought about it?"

"You mean work-life balance and all that shit?"

He placed his palm on her leg, sliding it up and down the slinky satin of the skirt. "What is your escape from acting? What recharges your creative well? How do you take a break from it?"

"I work out."

Nova huffed a laugh. "Where's the fun? The spontaneity? I mean, if I come to see you, will you be present? Or will I be tucked away in a trailer while you're on set, then be waiting for you while you work out in the hours you aren't filming. Don't you want to learn guitar, go hiking, sit and read a book while rain hits the windows?"

Presley looked at her as if she was talking a foreign language.

"I wish you could see the look on your face. This isn't a hard concept."

He sat back in his chair and folded his arms. "Gimme a minute to think."

He closed his eyes, and she sipped her champagne while he sat, looking to all others as if he'd fallen asleep.

"Okay," he said, finally, opening his eyes. "I've got it. I'd like to volunteer. Something hands-on that gets me outside. Building houses. Disaster cleanup. I don't do anything good beyond writing checks and it gets old. Perhaps be a spokesperson for something noble. The UN. I don't know. Something good."

"That's a good one. Something not about you. The first seems easier than the second, but I'm sure you know actors who already work for the UN in some way. Maybe they could make introductions for you. What about something fun?"

"Travel. There are so many places of the world I haven't been. Perhaps we can go see them together when we get a chance."

Nova smiled. "Why don't we plan it instead of hoping for it? Look at the next block of time in your schedule where you aren't filming. Where would you want to go first?"

"First. I'd love a luxury hotel somewhere beautiful, like the Society Islands. Tahiti. Bora Bora. I need some serious rest."

"Then that's where we'll go."

Presley cupped her cheek. "You make it sound so simple."

"It is. Because we make it so."

He kissed her softly. "What about you?"

Nova smiled. "My resolution is to lie on a beach in Bora Bora with you."

"That's a cheat of an answer."

"Okay. So, I guess my resolutions would be to step out of my comfort zone a little more. Do something that exhilarates me."

"Doing you exhilarates me."

Nova nearly choked on her glass of champagne. "Presley," she warned.

"What? If we're talking New Year's resolutions, my goal is to do you as many times as humanly possible. Just being honest. But what did you have in mind?"

What *did* she have in mind? "This year was all about moving onto the boat. Finishing renovating it, decorating it, and moving on board. Getting comfortable being by myself, finding community on the canals. And it was a big leap. Now that's all done, I see how it could all become repetitive. Maybe travel is it. Maybe letting you finally whip me into shape is it, seeing I'm going to be around you a lot more."

"Maybe it's sending your poetry out on submission to talented editors at big publishing houses or finding a freelance editor you trust and self-publishing them yourself. Maybe it's placing a bet on your career. Placing a bet on us. Placing a bet on you."

Her jaw opened, but words didn't automatically come out. She repeated the action then realised she probably looked like an overdressed goldfish. "Okay."

"Okay to all of it?"

Nova sucked in a big breath of air. If she put it out into the universe, she was going to have to do it. She couldn't renege. "Yes, I'm going to put my poetry out into the world in some fashion."

"And?"

"I'm going to place a bet on us. We'll travel and make homes in two countries. I don't even know what paperwork that all involves to travel. But I'll do it."

Presley grinned. "I'm pleased to hear that. But what about the biggest part of all that?"

"Which part?"

"The part where you bet on yourself. You're talented and

smart. I've always thought the name Nova suited you because you're like a supernova. You're brighter than the sun and have so much energy. I want to see you pour all that out into the world and see how big of an impact you could have. Because it will be massive, Nov. I know it."

The faith he had in her shook her. "I have my most recent poetry notebook here with me. In my case. I always travel with it in case I get inspired. As lovely as all this is, would you like to go back and read it?"

Presley stood and offered her his hand. "Damn straight I would. I'll do you a swap. I'll let you read the script for the role I really want, so you can see why it means so much to me."

"Are you meant to do that?" she asked as he led her out of the building and into a waiting black cab.

"The Savoy, please," he said to the driver as he helped her climb inside. Once seated, he took her hand. "No. I'm not meant to. But if I can't trust you, then I've got no one."

She placed her hand to his cheek when they finally set foot in the hotel elevator. "Can I ask you a huge favour?"

"Anything, babe."

"Before we settle down and read, will you make love to me first?"

Presley smiled. "I was kind of hoping that would be the order of events."

When the elevator doors closed, he pressed her back to the green walls, gathered her hands over her head in one fist, and kissed as if it had been years since they last touched, not moments in the cab.

Her body melted against his. In her heels, she was fractionally closer to him in height, but not enough to line up where she needed him most, leaving her empty and needy.

“Presley,” she groaned as his lips kissed a trail down her cheek, along her ear.

As the doors opened, he swept her into his arms and carried her the short distance to the suite. He fumbled getting the key from his pocket, but they managed to get through the door. He ignored the gorgeous tan sofa and the lights of the buildings reflecting onto the Thames and strode straight to their bed.

Without turning on the lights, he carefully removed his own mask and then hers, before reaching for the zipper of her dress. The only sound in the room was their breath and the sound of metal teeth coming apart as his fingers trailed down her back. “Maybe we were supposed to wait for this,” he said before nipping the side of her neck playfully.

“What do you mean?” she asked, pushing his newly acquired suit jacket off his shoulders.

“You and me.” He captured her hands and held them behind her back. “Maybe the reason this didn’t happen sooner was because it wasn’t meant to. We were meant to have all those other experiences we’ve had without each other, so we’d be ready to be with each other now. It was meant to happen this Christmas.”

“I like that idea, Presley.”

He kissed her softly. “Yeah. So do I.”

15

PRESLEY

Presley let go of Nova's hands and brushed her dress from her shoulders, nudging it over her frame as it dropped to the floor. He indulged himself by dipping his head to suck one of her braless nipples into his mouth.

"Pres," Nova gasped, weaving her fingers into his hair to hold him there. Yeah, small but highly sensitive breasts were now his crack. In her panties and heels, with her hair up in a messy riot, she looked every inch the pinup.

"As much as I love this," he said, touching the ends of her hair, "I want to watch you take it down."

He sat on the chaise at the bottom of the bed and leaned back, unbuttoning his shirt lazily.

Nova smiled softly as she raised her hands to her hair and began removing the hair clips holding it up. Black lace panties sat low on her hips; her legs looked long in the black strappy heels.

Using his palm, he nudged his hard dick into a more comfortable position, then undid the belt, buttons, and zipper. But all the while he watched her until her hair tumbled free.

"Your hair is one of the prettiest things about you," he said. "Suits your name."

Nova smiled and glanced over to the window where the curtains were open.

"No one can see us," he reassured. "It's dark in here."

Dropping to her knees, Nova crawled to the spot between his knees and slid both of her palms along his thighs until they brushed up either side of his dick, causing him to gasp. "Steady, Nov."

She grinned up at him and ran her tongue over her lower lip. She reached for the waistband of his trousers and boxer briefs and, with his help, tugged them from beneath him. The sight of her tongue sliding up his length had him leaking. But instead of sucking him like he'd expected, she returned to his shoes, undoing each one and removing his socks, before sliding his trousers and boxer briefs off fully.

The anticipation was killing him.

When she finally returned her lips to him, he reached for her hair, holding it out of the way so he would watch every kiss she placed on him. Her warmth breath made him shiver.

But nothing prepared him for the sight of her holding his dick and sucking it into her warm mouth. He'd not given her the chance to go down on him, always so eager to get her off and then plunge deep inside her. But this. He arched his back and inhaled deeply as he tried to get a grip on his self-control. The need to thrust into her mouth, to hold her in place while he fucked her mouth. It would all come in their future, but for now, her quiet exploration of him was perfect.

Her head began to bob as she took him deeper, as she

introduced her hand and saliva to slide along his length from balls to tip.

"Fuck," he groaned, enjoying it too much to stop, even though he should real soon.

When she twisted her palm as she moved, he gripped her wrist and hauled her to her feet and made short work of removing her panties. "I was enjoying that," she said.

"So was I. Too much. Ride me, babe."

Nova grinned and lowered herself over him, her knees just on the edge of the chaise. "Presley," she gasped.

Just as she bottomed out on him, he pushed himself to his feet with her in his arms. As he'd hoped, she wrapped her legs around his waist and locked her feet as he thrust up into her.

"Am I not too heavy?" she whispered in his ear.

He chuckled. "I deadlift the equivalent to three of you."

"Oh."

"Yeah. So, shut up and kiss me."

She cupped his cheeks and did as he said, throwing herself into the kiss and trusting him to hold her while she did so. And the last parts of him—the parts that said it was too much, too fast, the wrong time—all disappeared, leaving him fully in the moment with her.

"You know I love you," he said against her lips.

Her smile told him the answer before her words. "I do. You know I love you too, right?"

"That makes me the luckiest guy in the world." He carried her to the bed, and gently laid her down, still inside her. "You wanted to make love, yeah?"

"Yes."

That he could do. He set a slow and almost desperate pace, feeling every inch of her as she grew wetter around him. With one hand holding her hands above her head, and the other gently holding the back of her knee up against his ribs, he withdrew every inch of his cock before sliding back inside her until they were both gasping.

His control was fraying.

His orgasm was so close.

He slid his hand beneath her butt, tilting her hips so he could hit that spot deep inside her that seemed to detonate when they came together.

Presley," she gasped. "Oh, God. I'm so . . . close."

He buried his head against her neck, kissing her softly. "Me too," he said, screwing his eyes shut tightly as he focused on the balance between them. So close to the tipping point himself, but desperate to share it with Nova.

The blissful tightening started in his balls. "Shit, Nov. Come with me," he begged.

As soon as he felt her tighten around him and her the gasp of air leave her lips, he let go of control and pumped hard into her, joining her as they fell over the edge together.

"Babe," he groaned, unable to so anything but immerse himself in the feel of the two of them as he throbbed deep inside her.

Her arms tightened around him, her fingertips digging into his shoulders, holding him close. Neither of them moved, although he did take some of his weight into his elbows so he wouldn't crush her.

"Every time it gets better," he mumbled into the pillow.

"Practice makes perfect," Nova said playfully.

"You saying it's not perfect, babe?"

"It was perfect yesterday, and even more perfect today."

Presley smiled and kissed her neck before lifting to kiss her lips. "I look forward to tomorrow being even more perfect than today."

Slowly, he withdrew from her, feeling his cum leak

between them. He should probably give a shit about the bedding, but seeing he'd paid fourteen grand for the suite, he didn't. Instead, he got a perverse sense of satisfaction out of it.

"What are you thinking about with that smile?"

"You don't want to know."

"I do."

He shrugged his shoulders. "Just thinking how amazing it felt to have not used a condom and for everything to leak onto the bedding at the end. It's hot."

Nova's chuckle turned into a belly laugh. "You're right. I shouldn't have asked."

He reached for her hand and tugged her toward the bathroom. "Let's shower all this off us, order the best comfort food we can find on the menu, and then read, yeah?"

An hour later, they were both sat on the bed, wrapped in thick white robes. Nova took a bite of her burger then wiped her fingers on her napkin before turning a page of his script. He watched her eyes flick across the lines.

"What?" she said, without looking up.

"What what?"

"I can feel you watching me."

He waited for her to look at him. "First, I wondered how you can shovel away so much food and never put on any weight."

"Fast revving metabolism." She popped a salty fry in her mouth. "Those fancy meals are never filling. All show and no substance. Don't give me foamed this and whisper of that. I need potatoes and salt. What was second?"

"Second. This is fucking heartbreakingly beautiful, Nov." He looked down at the poem that had taken his breath away. "In the silence, a thousand unspoken words and touches. In the silence, a two of us that could have been. In the silence, my fleeting chance at happiness. A happiness that will never be because of him."

Nova blushed, her cheeks turning a cute pink. "Thank you."

"You can feel the longing. And in that one about loss, about feeling buried without having died. It's so visceral. The words you choose. And even the words you don't choose. The bits you leave out. Like nothing is overdescribed. I don't know how else to explain. They're beautiful and haunting and emotive. You have a real talent."

She dipped three fries into the ketchup but paused. "You really think so?"

He climbed to his knees. "I do. Narmin's sister is with a publisher in New York. Why don't we ask Narmin to connect you?"

"I'm a freelance copy editor for some of the New York publishing houses. I know how it all works and can do it myself. We don't need to ask Narmin when she is already doing so much for you."

"Sorry. I didn't mean to suggest you didn't. I guess I'm just proud of you, and excited that you might get the chance to put this out in the world for everyone else to read. And I wanted to help you get there."

Nova smiled, popped the fries in her mouth, then pushed the plate away so she could reach him. He placed his own dishes on the floor and then took her notebook and his script and placed them on the bedside table.

"Thank you," she said, finally. "And I can see why you want this part so badly. It's a great role and so well written. It's hard to even imagine how horrifying these experiences are for the main character. I had no idea this was based on a true story."

Presley glanced down at his watch. "We missed the countdown. It's two in the morning. Happy New Year, Nov. Let's hope we both get what we wish for."

"I hate what happened to get you to come to my boat. But I'm so glad you did. What you said earlier about timing? And us having to wait until now to get together for reasons that might not ever make sense? Maybe that applies to both of these projects, but I'm really glad you're here with me now for the ride."

"Me too." He tugged her tight. "Are you tired?"

"I just ate a burger and fries, so no."

He rearranged them both until his head was propped up against pillows with Nova tucked beneath his arm. "In that case, let's see if we can find a movie to watch to help us fall asleep."

And as Nova passed out as while Arnold Schwarzenegger mumbled about being back, he realised he hadn't thought about what was waiting for him back in Hollywood all evening.

16

NOVA

"Nov, have you seen my headphones?" Presley asked as he tossed cushions around on the sofa two hours after they arrived back on the boat from London, having picked Minerva up from the cattery on the way. They'd had an early brunch, then a smooth ride home in the limo where Nova had dozed against Presley's shoulder.

She lit the fire as Minerva continued to ignore her. Instead, the cat trotted after Presley like a long-lost lover returned.

Like all women do, she thought with a huff. Second looks from women had always been something she'd dealt with, but before, she'd had no skin in the game in keeping his attention. Their time in London had gone a long way to reassure her that if Presley did notice the women, he certainly wasn't flirting or doing anything to suggest their relationship was anything other than rock solid.

Over the last week, his things had all merged with hers. She'd combined her sweaters into one of the drawers beneath her bed and hidden his suitcase in the gap behind the drawers. It had helped make the whole thing feel less transitory. Like there wasn't a moment coming where she'd have to say goodbye and put him on an airplane.

"Did you check the shelf opposite the bed?

"Yeah. They've probably dropped down the back of something. Do you mind if I take this video call with my agent without them?"

Nova looked down at the beef that was sizzling in a large pan on the gas. "I can pause the chili while you take it and go to the bedroom and read to give you some privacy."

Presley shook his head. "I don't mind you hearing it, just didn't want to annoy you."

Figuring out how to coexist at this new spot in their relationship felt easy. She'd miss him when he left.

"Don't worry about me. I'm fine. I'll try to keep the banging to a minimum."

Presley grinned. "I kind of like when you're banging."

"Perv. Get on with your call."

Within moments, she heard the nasally American drawl of Narmin, a name Nova had heard often, but a person whom she'd never met. Her rare visits to Los Angeles from England had never overlapped with Narmin's visits from New York.

With the beef browned, she began to add all the other ingredients. Cans of plump kidneys beans and her secret ingredient, a can of Heinz baked beans. Juicy tomatoes, red wine vinegar, mustard, chilli powder, Worcestershire sauce, and other seasonings went in next. As she stirred in the bacon she'd fried and chopped, she heard snatches of the conversation.

Coverage isn't dying down as we expected.

Wouldn't be as bad if you were aiming at the male-led action market, but the Oscar market's more delicate.

Nova rolled her eyes. Deep down, she understood what Narmin was saying, but she just wished it wasn't true.

When the pot came to the boil, she poured it into a casserole dish, and, using oven gloves, carried it over to the compartment above the fire where it could slow cook for hours until they were ready for dinner.

"Anyway," Narmin continued. "We have a great plan. Winona Rae who is scheduled to play the lead female role and love interest in the movie, just found out her boyfriend cheated on her with his co-star and wants a contract bounce-back relationship."

Nova looked over at Presley and scrunched up her nose. "That's awful," she mouthed.

Presley nodded.

"Her agent was one of my protégés, so I got in touch, figured we could help each other out. So, when you get back, you and her are going to enter a contract relationship. It's all laid out. She'll meet you from the airport, we'll make sure a photographer is there to snap it, so make sure it looks realistic. Gossip columnist Dante De León is poised to the get the big reveal."

Nova's stomach clenched as surely as if invisible arms had gripped her. Dante ran one of those trash gossip sites that had a bazillion followers. But the idea of him pretending to be with someone else . . .

Presley's eyes went wide. "I can't do that. I have a girlfriend."

"Since when?" Narmin yelled. "You were banging two chicks on camera five minutes ago."

"There's video?"

"You know what I mean . . . and no, no video to the best of my knowledge, or they would have shared it when the headlines calmed down. This is all about rebuilding your credibility. The producers and Hattie see the chemistry between you and Winona, they're going to forget all about any other option. Gossip, speculation about whether sex scenes are real or not . . . it all adds to the mystery of the film making it bigger than it would have been. And I don't give a shit who you are giving it to, Presley. Trust me, you need to do this to salvage your reputation."

Presley reached out his hand for Nova and she walked to him and took it, gripping it tightly. "It's Nova, Narmin."

Narmin pursed her lips and scowled. "Honestly, Presley, you could be dating royalty and I'd still say what I'm about to say next. Winona Rae is a cert for the movie. The part was written specifically for her, and she would rather act with you. You want to quickly reassure the studio you are the right pick for the movie, you need to show them believable chemistry. No offence, Nova, but you're a big girl, and need to realise this is just a business deal and just the break Presley needs."

Presley flinched. "Don't dismiss her feelings like that, Narmin. Even if we weren't dating, I wouldn't be cool with that."

Narmin sighed. "Nova can wait, Presley. This opportunity can't. Think about it, get back to me tomorrow."

A frosty silence blanketed the boat in contrast to the racing thoughts in Nova's mind. The world he lived in was so complex and foreign to her own. She escaped into words, lived simply. And Presley, after being taken advantage of, was being told his best career move, to protect the movie he really wanted to do, was to pretend to love someone else.

"Shit," Presley said, tugging a hand through his hair before standing and marching to the fridge. He yanked the door open, grabbed a bottle of white wine he bought at a wine merchant's near their hotel, opened it, and poured them both a large glass. When he sat back down next to her, he handed her the other glass.

"Do you want to do it?" Nova asked.

"Honestly? If this had been an option three weeks ago, I would probably have stayed in Los Angeles and started planning it out. It's the perfect solution. But I won't disrespect you and us like that. I'll tell her no." But the way he leaned forward and tugged at his hair, the strain on his face, and the way he shook his head and sighed told her everything she needed to know. He'd been offered an out by Narmin, but he didn't feel like he could take it.

Because of her.

Nova took a large gulp, allowing the likely very expensive wine to burn her throat. Thoughts raced. It was acting, right? Did it mean anything to the two of them? But would that acting turn into something more? What if spending time together progressed into something real?

"Is this something that happens a lot?" she asked. It sounded so ludicrous to her ears, but maybe it wasn't such a foreign concept to actors.

"All the time. It helps to build hype for the movie. Or sometimes, it could be because an actor has social anxiety, and appearing on the press junket as a couple just makes life easier for that person. I'm sorry Narmin was so disrespectful to you. I'll talk to her about it."

"No," she said, placing her hand on his arm. "She's just looking out for you."

"Not if she's suggesting I do this even after I told her were dating."

Nova took another gulp of wine to steady her nerve for what she was about to say. "You need to do it."

Presley looked at her as if she was losing her mind. "What? No. That's the worst idea."

"Narmin only suggested it because she thought you were single. That status changed in a week. A week, Presley. She wasn't to know. And . . . it's just acting right. It would be like a live-action movie. Theatre is perhaps a better analogy. I can . . . at least, I think I can get my head around that."

"Nov," Presley said, his voice almost tortured.

"Promise me it will be acting," she whispered.

He took their wine glasses and placed them on the television unit before pulling her onto his lap and burying his face in her hair. "I don't want to do it if it hurts you or us in any way. No movie is worth that."

"Then, that's your choice." She hugged him tightly. "But if this movie means that much to you, and is the opportunity of a lifetime you really want, then maybe you should do it."

"I'll find another way, Nov."

But the more he pushed back, the more she buried the lead weight in her gut and became determined he should.

"I have to be okay with you making out with other people as part of your job. Maybe okay is the wrong word, but I can't get jealous every time and get all bent out of shape that you're knocking boots with someone on screen. I trust you, to not spend a minute more than you need to, to not do stupid shit like stay over at each other's houses, because I think that's a hard limit for me."

Presley looked up at her, his eyes wide, as if someone had just handed him the thing at the very top of his Christmas list. "You'd be cool with this?"

She sighed. "I'm telling you that I think I can handle it, because I know how much this role means to you. Best case, we hide what we are to each other, worst case . . . we put this on hold while you—"

"No, there is no 'on hold' with this. We talk. We stick

with our plan. We see each other every other week. Weave into the narrative that Winona is perfectly cool with me hanging out with my best friend."

"Okay."

"Okay?" Presley cupped her cheeks. "You're making it sound like this is easy."

"It's not easy, Presley. Right now, I'm holding onto my sanity by reassuring myself that you haven't let me down as a friend in two decades beyond moving across an ocean away from me. I'd like to think you'd treat your girlfriend even better."

"I will, I promise."

"If this is the career you want, if this is the role worth betting it all on, then we fight this shit together, right?"

Presley took a deep breath, and she felt his shoulders sag. "I don't know why I waited this long for this, Nov. For you and me. But I'm so fucking glad I'm here now. That you're willing to help me pull this off so I can get what I want. The sacrifice is all yours."

She shook her head. "Not really. You don't want to be in this situation either. But here we are. It's how we respond to it that matters, right?"

Presley kissed her softly, then with more desire. His hands slid beneath her sweater, up her back, around her ribs.

And when he finally took her on the rug in front of the fire, she prayed she'd made the right choice.

17

PRESLEY

"Babe," Presley whispered, gently shaking Nova until she woke up.

He'd packed his things the previous evening, leaving them in the living room of the boat, and he'd silently crept out of bed to get dressed. The fire was lit, and he'd brought in more logs and kindling. The kettle was boiled, and a cup of tea was on the floor next to the bed. Minerva was fed so she'd leave the two of them alone while he said his goodbyes.

Nova turned, her lips all soft. "You're leaving?"

He kissed her then ran a knuckle down her cheek. "I'll sort out tickets for you when I land, and I'll make sure you know every detail of things between me and Winona so nothing surprises you, should it make the media."

She ran a thumb over his lips. "Take care of yourself."

"You too. I'm not going to worry about you being on the canal on your own, because you were doing it before you were mine. But make sure nothing happens to my girlfriend. I happen to be deeply in love with her."

Nova smiled. "She happens to be in love with you too."

"Don't get out of bed," he said, opening the small narrow window on the side of the boat. "I'll lock up after I leave and drop the keys back through here, yeah?"

"Safe travels."

"Oh, and Nov. I don't hate Christmas, if it means I get to spend it like this, with you." With one last kiss that was difficult to end, he left the boat.

It was only fourteen hours later, when the pilot of the private jet told him they were an hour outside of LA, did he turn his mind to what would happen next. He'd spent the flight alternately looking at the script and thinking of Nova. In between, he'd napped and hydrated.

He stepped into the private bathroom on the plane and cleaned himself up. He'd been told to wear something navy. Winona was going to wear deep blue pants with an orange stripe down the side and a white sweater, all designer label, so they would coordinate. He'd also been told to avoid anything remotely seasonal, not that he ever wore it anyway. But they needed the photographs to be evergreen that could be circulated through January and February.

He looked at himself in the mirror and felt . . .

Sick.

Nervous.

"It's just acting, right?" he said, his whispered voice drowned out by the dull roar of the jet's engines.

He needed to be more convincing. He pulled on the navy cashmere sweater he'd bought the day before over his head, imagining it was part of his costume.

It's just acting.

His hair needed a trim, but he damped it down and styled it a little different to normal.

Yeah, it felt better when he felt like he was slipping into

a role. The role of an actor whose prize project was on the line.

As soon as he got a signal on his phone, he texted Nova.

Just landing. Miss you already.

By the time he'd collected his bags and was ready to disembark, she'd replied.

Miss you too. Although there is now more room on the sofa again. Love you.

Love you to, he typed.

There are two 'o's in too.

Her reply made him grin. *Thank you Ms. Copy Editor.*

He stepped off the jet into the private airport lounge, realising how utterly ridiculous his new setup was. The woman he loved was an ocean away, pretending she wasn't his girlfriend, while Winona was there, waiting for him to pretend she was. She stood when he walked into the terminal.

He was on full alert. It was weird to know there was someone planted to take pictures of you that you couldn't see.

"Hey," Winona said, a huge smile on her face. Her makeup was perfect and her hair in a messy ponytail that had likely been styled over two hours to look like that.

"Hey," he said, wondering where his improvisation skills had gone. He put his bags down and hugged her, way more intimately than you should hug a person you don't know. But his only thought was her head didn't fit against him properly like Nova's did. "Thanks so much for agreeing to this," he muttered.

She rubbed his back. "No problem. I really preferred our screen test together."

His heart began to race. Like he was on stage and

suddenly couldn't remember the next line. Except he could. He was meant to kiss her.

It's a role. It's a role.

But all he was capable of was a chaste kiss, to the left of her mouth with pursed lips, hidden by his hands that cupped her cheeks. And even that felt like cheating on Nova.

As if sensing he was bent out of shape, Winona took his hand. "Get your bags, let's get in my car, and I'll drive you home so we can chat about how to do this."

Presley smiled. The Hollywood one that Nova teased him about. The one without dimples. He would save those for her.

As they left the building, he heard the click of the camera. "Don't you have something better to do than stalk people?" he shouted.

"Sorry, Mr. James. Just doing my job."

"A job we organised," Winona whispered as she unlocked her car. A flashy silver sports car.

"He doesn't need to know Narmin sent the tip in."

She opened the trunk, and he threw in his cases before rolling up his sleeves. Compared to the wet and cold Welsh canal, it was positively balmy. He grabbed his sunglasses from their case and slipped them on. "You want to drive?" she asked, dangling the keys. "Would probably look more stereotypically pleasing to the ladies. And would also totally piss my ex off. I never let him drive my car."

Presley remembered that Winona had been such a huge part of why he'd wanted the role. Talented actor. Fun to be around.

And most definitely not Nova.

He missed his little sea witch. Or canal witch, which sounded way less mysterious.

Already after one event, he wasn't sure he could do this.

"Sure." He took the keys, adjusted the seat, and got comfortable. As he pulled out of the airport, he realised the photographer was following close behind. Trying to see where he was headed.

When he finally pulled into his driveway forty minutes later, he realised he owned bricks and mortar, but didn't own a home. He wondered what Nova would make of the lack of Christmas decorations. Not so much as a wreath or bauble. As the gates closed behind him, he breathed a sigh of relief. Within three seconds, no one would be able to see him.

It sucked that he was now obliged to spend enough time with Winona for it to be believable. "Given we were followed, we should probably hang out for a while longer."

"Sure. Want to take a walk or go grab coffee or something? I have some shorts I can change into."

He led them into his house, which already felt sacrilegious. It should be Nova stepping into it with him. He'd promised her he wouldn't let the woman sleep over, but even changing her clothes felt weird under the premise of the two of them pretending to be involved.

And, God, thinking of Nova made him miss her more powerfully than he ever had before.

"I'm starved. There's a great Italian just down Sunset Boulevard. Want to grab an early lunch?"

Winona laughed. "Are you kidding? I haven't even sniffed Italian food in seven years. I only need to look at a bowl of pasta and I gain ten pounds."

Nova would have raced him out of the door for a good carbonara. "Okay, just a quick coffee then. We can figure this shit out."

Winona nodded. "Would love to."

Once at the coffee shop, he'd nudged her in the direction of a dark corner, but she reminded him the point was to be seen. Winona tugged her sweater over her head. Beneath it, she wore one of those camisole tops that could be construed as innocuous but was ivory silk and a had a deep lace-edged V. Beneath it, perky nipples attached to gravity-defying augmented breasts revealed the lack of a bra.

She'd obviously read the memo on how to get your contract relationship nudged up the social media interest charts.

"I hope this works out," she said. "I really wasn't kidding when I said I preferred our screen test. I heard Cameron Kelly can also be a real dick to work with. All method acting, treating his co-star like his character. And lord knows I don't want to be bossed about by a self-absorbed egotist when the cameras aren't rolling."

Presley relaxed for the first time since he'd disembarked the private jet. "Thanks for the compliment, and yeah, I've worked with a couple of method actors. It can be really hard on the rest of the cast."

"No kidding. I need to get to know the person I'm working with to do my best work. When you know someone, you can be more vulnerable and trust them to be with you in the moment. But you can't get to know someone when they pretend they are Abraham Lincoln every time you talk."

Which was weird. Because wasn't this all one giant long method acting experiment? Pretending twenty-four seven he was in a relationship with her. Realising the car with the photographer was on the opposite side of the street, he reached across the table for Winona's hand. Her fingers were cool, unlike Nova's perpetually warm skin.

It didn't feel right, but he'd process those thoughts later. For now, he'd act.

"Don't you feel it's ridiculous that we have to do this?" he asked.

"Do what? Have coffee?"

He shook his head. "No. Pretend."

"It's what we do, right? Pretend. But . . ." Winona raised his fingers to her lips and kissed them gently. "We're both consenting adults. If lines get blurred, it's not the end of the world. And to be honest, I want to punch my ex in the throat instead of taking the high road by putting out statements saying I wish him well."

Her lips on his fingers felt treacherous. Were her lines already blurred? Was the look in her eyes real or was she still acting? He couldn't tell.

"I have a girlfriend," he said, hoping that would cut off any further conversation.

"Of course," Winona said, her smile so bright it looked fragile.

Thirty-six hours later, standing on a red carpet for a movie release Winona had been involved in, he knew he was in trouble. He'd stepped out of their limo and offered her his hand while thousands of cameras flashed at them, and she'd been . . . more.

More affectionate. More touchy-feely. More lingering gazes. She'd kissed him chastely. It was, after all, going to hit every major entertainment news media. All of it within the boundaries they'd discussed. But he felt treacherous. And wretched. And a whole bunch of other words Nova would probably use instead of saying she felt like shit.

Because that's how he felt.

Like shit.

At the end of the movie, where Winona had been brilliant but the plot dull, he excused himself and hid in a toilet cubicle for ten minutes to calm his panic.

Once he felt calmer and had made the decision to tell both Winona and Narmin he couldn't keep this up, he walked out of the bathroom, a stupid term for just a toilet and sink, and bumped straight into Hattie Lee.

"Hattie," he said, steadying her. "Shit. I'm sorry. I didn't hurt you did I?"

Hattie shook her head but raised her eyebrow.. "No, I'm okay. I saw you were here with Winona."

There came a time in every man's life when he could lie to get himself out trouble in the moment or tell the truth and be able to live with himself for the rest of his life. "It's not what you think."

"No?"

"We're friends. And to be honest, I was hoping you'd see us together and see the chemistry we had. But I can't do it. Which I know probably makes you think I'm a shit actor as well as a shit human being too. But here's the thing. I used to think there was pretty much nothing I wouldn't do to work with you because I've been typecast into a box I can't seem to break free from. I feel like working with you would make me the best actor I could be. Because I think you and this movie you're trying to make are both incredible. But it's morally bankrupt to pretend." Presley tugged his hand through his hair. He was blowing this. Narmin was going to kill him. "I made a stupid mistake, Hattie. An error of judgement. But my best friend forgave me. And that's all that matters because I love her. And I was about to betray that by pretending I'm something I'm not to impress you. I've learned from my mistake. I love Nova. If none of that's enough for you to put me in this movie, I understand."

Unable to think of anything else to say, he hurried to

Winona's side, waiting while she schmoozed the crowd. And when she was done and they were bundled into the limo home, he told her what he'd told Hattie.

She'd understood.

And once he'd dropped her at her door, he called Nova, needing to speak to her.

But she didn't answer.

Nor did she answer when he tried again an hour later.

Climbing into bed, he realised he'd lost a bunch of things that night. Narmin's faith in him. His fake relationship. His movie role. The one thing he prayed he hadn't lost, was Nova.

18

NOVA

Under the inky-blue night sky, Nova pressed the gate buzzer repeatedly. The Santa Ana winds whipped up dust around her, and, quite frankly, she'd had enough of . . . well . . . everything.

Presley had sounded unhappy when he'd called her after his first day with Winona. And the only thing stopping the two of them being together right now while he navigated all this was Nova's pride. So, she'd whipped out her credit card, found a budget seat where she'd spent the last miserable ten hours, and made the trip to see him. Except, it was now nearly three in the morning, because lost luggage, a maintenance problem, a dead phone, and a crew shortage meant nothing at the airport had gone smoothly.

"Hello?" Presley said gruffly, half asleep.

"If you don't let me in within five seconds, I'm going to pass out beneath this ginormous bush, and you can find me in the morning."

"Nov?" She heard sheets rustling. "You're outside?"

"And likely to die of exhaustion right by your gates if you don't open them."

"Here." The clanking sound of the gate mechanism made her jump. "On my way."

The gates began to rattle on their tracks and open. The yard hadn't changed. Although using the word *yard* for something that looked a little like a Japanese botanical garden was a poor word choice. It was precise, and so not Presley. But she was too tired to properly admire the round shrubs, concrete balls, and perfectly manicured trees that looked like souped-up bonsai.

She was almost to the top of the drive when the front door opened and a slightly rumpled Presley in nothing but jeans he hadn't taken the time to fasten yanked the door open. He rubbed his hands over his face, his eyes, his hair.

"Fuck. It really is you," he said, tugging her into his arms, fisting her hair in his hand. He buried his nose against her neck, not even kissing her, just holding her tight. That alone was proof enough she'd made the right decision. "How? Why did . . . ? Shit. I don't even care. I'm just so glad you're here."

While she didn't want to let him go or step away from his comforting scent and heat, she stepped back. "We probably shouldn't be doing this given the ruse you and Winona are pulling, right?"

"Oh, right." Presley looked around her at the gate, which was slowly rumbling closed. "Come in."

He took her hand and led her inside. The house was just as bland as she remembered it. All neutrals with a splash of tan here and there.

Presley cupped her cheeks and kissed her like he hadn't seen her in forever. Their tongues met, one of them sighed, and his arms did their best to hold her around her small backpack.

"Why don't you have any luggage?" he asked.

Nova yawned, then answered. "It's currently enjoying the baggage network in New York. I changed planes. My bags, however, did not. I have nothing beyond my laptop, cables, headphones, and a magazine."

He stroked his thumb along her jaw. "We'll find them. And we'll find you clothes to wear until we do."

"Right now, as sexy as your body is, I just want to go to bed. I probably should shower, but I can't be arsed. My body knows it's missed breakfast in England, but I'm too tired to care."

Presley took her hand. "Bed works. So does sleep. I can make love to you and clean you up afterwards in the morning."

"That might be the hottest thing you've said."

"Making love?"

Nova huffed a laugh. "No, that it can all wait."

Presley grinned and led her past the room she'd slept in on previous visits. Once in his own room, he cupped her cheeks and kissed her lips softly. "I'm glad you're here. And we can chat in the morning, yeah?"

Nova slid her backpack off her shoulders, and Presley helped her make quick work of the rest of her clothes before slipping one of his T-shirts over her head. He slipped off his jeans and then lifted the rumpled sheets on his bed so she could climb beneath them.

"This bed is huge," she mumbled, as he tugged the sheet over her.

Presley climbed in on the other side but pulled her close. "We're still sleeping like this," he said, snaking his arms around her before burying his head in her hair. "Fuck, I missed this."

"It's only been three days."

"Still fucking missed it."

When she woke the following morning, she was alone. Not what she had expected at all. But just as she tried to sit up in bed, the bedroom door burst open and Presley, dressed, showered, and carrying bags, entered. He dropped them on the floor like he didn't give a shit. But bags with names like Agent Provocateur, Prada, and Chanel needed respect.

"What did you buy?" she said, suddenly realising he was stripping his clothes off.

"Shit you needed. Rodeo Drive was the closest place. Wanted to make sure I was back before you woke up." His T-shirt flew toward the bathroom, his jeans and boxer briefs dropped where he stood.

She should be mad. A quick trip to Gap would have sufficed, but instead she focused on the deep-set V that led to . . . well, guess he really did intend to make love to her.

Playfully, he clambered onto the bed, threw himself onto her, and scooped her into his arms, all the while nibbling on the side of her neck.

"Pres," she squealed as he flipped her onto her back, then hoisted her over his shoulder.

She slapped his bare-naked arse as he carried her to the bathroom, marching them both into the shower. A shower that was large enough to hold a dance party.

He turned the taps on, and water seemed to pour from everywhere. A huge overhead rain shower, and jets firing from the left and right.

Nova stepped into the melee of it and sighed as the water massaged her tired body. When she tipped her head back and let water sluice down her body, she held her breath so she could stay there for as long as possible.

When she finally needed air and stepped out of the

spray, she found Presley watching her intently, stroking himself. "Need help?" she asked.

Presley grinned. "Nope."

He dropped to his knees, grabbed one ankle, and lifted her leg over his shoulder. Nova slammed her hands to the shower wall and glass screen to hold herself upright. What the shower had eased, Presley tongue made taught again. Her body snapped back into savouring the feel of him as he circled her clit before sucking on it. A slow and steady lick and pull lured her into the easiest of orgasms that rattled through her body.

"I like your shower," she said breathlessly as he climbed to his feet.

Somehow, when they were naked like this, he felt bigger. Taller. More overpowering. And she wasn't embarrassed to admit she loved it.

"I like the way you come on my tongue, so we're even." He pressed his lips to hers. "Any objection to me fucking you in the shower right now and making love to you later?"

Nova grinned, then turned around to face the wall, pressing her palms to the tile. "Like this?" she asked, looking over her shoulder at him.

Presley bit down on his lower lip. "Exactly like that." He stepped up to her, sliding his dick between her legs first, letting it rub against her already sensitive clit. "That feels good."

With water pounding the two of them, Nova turned her gaze between her legs, opening them a little wider.

Presley took the hint and, bending his knees, eased his cock into her.

Even on her toes, it was difficult to manage the height difference.

"Shit," Presley cursed. "Knees, babe."

And she did as he said, dropping to the cool tile. Presley followed her, running his palm over her wet skin. Her body was on fire for him.

"Please," she gasped.

He placed his palms either side of her own. "You want this?" His voice was raw with need.

"Yes." The word was filled with desperation. She pressed back against his thighs, willing him to take her.

Presley leaned up, and, with one hand, slid into her hard.

They groaned in unison.

Sometimes, the size of him was on the verge of being too much. And it was everything she wanted.

Unable to control himself, Presley began to take her hard. She might get bruises on her knees later, but she didn't want to miss a single delicious second as he thrust into her, his grunts echoing around the bathroom.

"Fuck," he growled. "Feels so good. Not hurting you am I?"

She lowered her arms to the tile and placed her forehead on them, arching her back. "Not at all. Just don't stop."

And he didn't. The thrill of being taken so roughly pushed her swiftly to a second orgasm.

"I can feel that, Nov. Oh . . . fuck . . . "

He slammed into her, holding her hips so tightly she couldn't move, but could feel him pulsing inside her. When he was done, he fell forward over her, kissing her shoulders softly.

"Jesus, babe. I'm sorry." He gently slid out of her, then clambered to his feet before lifting her gently to her own. He glanced down at her knees, inspecting them, before taking her chin between his thumb and finger. "Are you okay? That was . . ."

"Everything? Intense? Perfect?"

He studied her eyes. "Yeah." He kissed her softly. "All of that."

"You won't break me, Presley. And in case I wasn't clear, I really enjoyed that."

Presley grinned and led them both back beneath the shower spray. "Could you be any more perfect?"

They finished getting ready, Nova finally getting to see everything he'd bought for her. Outrageously expensive and gorgeous underwear that Presley had threatened to rip straight off her. A pretty sundress, some jeans, a jacket, and a striped sweater.

"You just sounded so . . . I don't know . . . lonely," Nova said when they finally sat to eat breakfast. "I didn't want you to have to go through this alone."

"Well," Presley said between mouthfuls of grapefruit. "I don't think we need to worry. I'm not doing the movie, and I'm not faking a relationship with anyone. I blew that up last night."

Nova paused with her toast halfway to her mouth. "What?"

Presley shrugged, but she could see the worry etched in his eyes. "It just all felt wrong. I already felt shitty about the way things had happened, and this was just prolonging it, making it worse. And then I almost bumped into Hattie Lee, and I ended up telling her how it sucked and why I wanted the role. And I told Winona I was sorry, but it was not for me."

"Shit."

"Yup."

"So, we move on," Nova said. "Courage, wisdom, justice, or temperance?"

"Wisdom. It was the right thing to do. Courage. I need to stand by my decision, regardless of the outcome."

Nova nodded. "Perfect. So, let's go for a walk by the beach in these ridiculously expensive clothes."

Presley's phone interrupted their conversation. He looked at the name. "I need to take this. I left Narmin a voicemail at like three in the morning with what I'd done."

She squeezed his hand. "Courage and wisdom. Yeah?"

Presley nodded and answered.

She couldn't hear all the conversation, just the slightly tinny pitch of Narmin.

"She what?" Presley said, suddenly pushing the chair back to pace the kitchen. There was a pause. A longer one this time. "Okay. Sure. Text it to me . . . Yeah, yeah. I will. Bye."

Presley placed the phone down on the table, then pressed both palms to the smooth wooden surface.

"What happened?" Nova asked, unable to wait any longer.

Presley looked at her, shock written all over his face. "The role's mine."

"What? How?"

He let out a huge breath. "Apparently, how impassioned I was last night was just what she wanted to see in the role. And the fact my moral compass stopped me from making a big mistake was similar to something the character would do. She felt it showed I could step out of the corporate machine of Hollywood, something she wasn't sure I was capable of. Hattie didn't hate it. She loved it. She wants me to call her this afternoon."

Nova stood up and threw her arms around him. "That's amazing, Pres. Congratulations."

He wrapped his arms around her. "It's you. You're my lucky charm."

"Meh. Not really. This was all you."

"I love you, Nov."

"I love you too."

EPILOGUE

MARCH: THREE YEARS LATER

"And the Oscar for best supporting actor goes to . . . Presley James."

Presley had always imagined what this moment would feel like. The adulation of his peers, the carefully orchestrated music, the handshake with his co-star, the kiss from Nova.

He had a speech written, just in case. From all the buzz the movie had received when it came out, he felt he had as good a chance as any of the others in his category. He'd covered the basics. Thanking his cast and crew, the director, producer, studio, his agent, his manager, and the Academy. Then he'd thank Nova for . . . well, everything. He'd borrowed some lines from her latest published poetry anthology to make his point.

But instead of a kiss, she squeezed his hand so tightly he thought she might break one of his bones.

And instead of a feeling of adulation, he felt terrified to his very core.

Because instead of being in the auditorium, they were watching the whole thing on the television in the early hours of the morning in a delivery room in Bath. Where they'd been for three days as the whole will-the-baby-appear-early-or-not scenario had played out.

"Push, Nova," the doctor said from his position squarely between her legs.

"You . . . won," she forced out, her brow all sweaty. She'd officially been in labour for twelve hours, which made the fact he should be at the Oscars and not in a hospital room, because their baby wasn't due for another four weeks, utterly insignificant.

He worried about Nova. He worried about the health of their child who was too impatient to wait any longer.

"Turn it off, I don't care." And he didn't. Watching the woman who had stood by him throughout his life give birth to their first child was way more important than anything else in the world.

"Look how . . . pretty—shit, this hurts—Narmin looks."

The epidural, for whatever reason, hadn't worked properly. He'd plead for more medication for her. But Nova had assured him that she felt capable of what was being asked of her.

And he had no doubts she was. She'd been handling the whole thing like a champ.

He, on the other hand, was a mess.

No amount of pre-natal classes, breathing classes, and focus and meditation classes were helping. At one point, when he'd needed to pee so badly he dashed to the toilet, he'd smacked himself on the cheeks a few times and given himself a pep talk that if she could endure the pain, he could at least witness it without fainting.

"There's only one woman I'm interested in right now, and she's currently got my hand in a death grip while she performs a miracle."

"Sorry," she whispered.

"Don't be. I feel like we should be sharing the pain of this. Not you carrying it all on your own." He ran the damp paper towel over her forehead. "I love you."

"You won." She winced. Another powerful contraction was coming.

"I did. The day you agreed to let me kiss you in our canal boat." A canal boat they were heading back to when they got out of hospital. She'd turned down his offer of a private suite in a fancy LA hospital, preferring her child to be brought into the world in an NHS ward.

Their parents were waiting for news.

He thought back to the day she'd told him.

I'm pregnant, Pres. And before you get excited and do something stupid like propose, please don't. I don't ever want to wonder if you proposed because of the baby.

She'd been right. It was totally something he would have done.

"Sweet talker."

"Right, push again, and this time, really bear down," the doctor said. "Presley, help her lean forward like you did last time. One good push and we might be done."

Nova's eyes met his. He could see the fear and panic and wonder written in them. It likely matched his own. "You've got this, babe."

And in a blur, they did as the doctor asked, his part wholly insignificant but hopefully a little bit helpful. Neither of them paid any attention to Narmin on stage reading Presley's carefully written speech.

Instead, something way more precious than a golden statuette entered their lives with a wail.

"Congratulations, it's a boy."

He'd thought he understood how much he loved Nova.

But when their child was put on her chest, and she held him while Presley held her, his heart cracked open so wide it was as if something had detonated within it. Something that would outlast roles, movies, and even Oscars.

"You did it, Nov. I'm so fucking proud of you. He's beautiful." He kissed the top of her head, then offered their son his finger, feeling his heart drop through the floor and bounce back up again when tiny fingers wrapped around his.

"We need to take him now. Being a bit early, we need to triple check everything for you."

Nova's eyes filled with tears. "What if he's not okay?"

Presley tightened his hold on her. "He's going to be. I promise." Because he couldn't stand the thought of anything else.

"We should call him Oscar," Nova said.

Presley huffed a laugh, despite his fear. "No. That's pretentious. Some teacher or kid in the future will ask why he was called Oscar and he'll have to explain it was because he was born the night his dad won an Oscar. Let's stick with Astro James." The name he'd picked because it meant *of the stars*. Nova had been uncertain until he'd told her it reminded him of her, the other star he loved.

She shrugged. "I just want him to be healthy."

"Same, babe. Same."

"Everything looks great," the nurse said, placing Astro on Nova's chest. "Just needs to put a little weight on, but otherwise no obvious cause for concern."

While the staff were busy around them, Presley wrapped his arms around Nova again, trying to rein in the emotions flooding through him. Tears stung as he looked down at the face of the child they'd created. He wanted to hold him, feel his precious little body in his own arms. But after everything Nova had gone through, she deserved every moment she took with him. He kissed Nova softly. "You were a superhero."

"You think? Did I really hurt your hand?"

Presley shook his head. "Didn't feel a thing."

"Liar."

"Maybe I am, but in the big scheme of twelve hours of labour and delivery, a hand squeeze is quite possibly the least I owe you."

He took his phone from his pocket and snapped a couple of pictures of Astro, Nova, and the three of them. As he was snapping, a message came through from Narmin.

Look what I'm holding.

She was grinning, holding his Oscar.

"Can I hold him for a minute?" he asked Nova.

"Of course. Sorry, I was hogging him. Here."

Presley placed his phone on the bed, and reached for the little guy, swaddled in hospital blankets. "God, we made this, Nov. He's all ours."

Nova sighed and closed her eyes, a soft smile on her face. "We did. Is it time to sleep yet?"

"Can you just take a picture of me and him first?"

Nova picked up the phone and took a snap. When Nova and Astro were finally settled in their room, he sent the picture to Narmin.

Look what I'm holding, he typed, matching her message.

Nine months later, Presley settled Astro on his lap. "We're going to watch your mum's favourite film," he whispered as he handed the little guy his first bottle of the day, making sure his hold was solid. Before he'd grabbed Astro from his makeshift cot on the canal boat, he'd lit the fire and then securely locked the guard around it. It didn't give them much room to walk through the boat, but with Astro starting to pull himself up using furniture, and walking when holding onto something, it had become a necessity.

He'd made a pot of tea and opened the curtains in the living room. The fairy lights now twinkled around the small tree, but he'd ignored the mass of presents piled up on and around the dinette.

Then he'd grabbed Astro without waking Nova and crept into the living room to change his nappy and make up a bottle.

It might be Christmas morning, but Astro had given them both a run for their money. Waking at one, then three o'clock, then five. Usually, he was a good sleeper but teething and shifting time zones from LA to the UK had knocked his body clock off.

Presley's mum and Nova's mum and dad would be over later. He and Nova were cooking all the sides, but his mum was bringing the turkey, already cooked, given their oven wasn't big enough. She was also bringing Minerva, who, after Nova had tearfully concluded they shouldn't keep putting her in a cattery because it was convenient, now lived with Sally.

He grinned at the thought of how big their LA home and London apartment were, yet they still chose to stay here on the boat, squashing everyone in their tiny living space.

"How about we watch this, bud?" Presley pressed play.

Astro's eyes grew wide as the brass intro began. Sleigh bells kicked in, and Presley glanced toward the bathroom door, wondering how long it would take Nova to wake. Red titles appeared over snow covered Dickensian London streets. To his embarrassment, he found himself singing about thankful hearts and a sea of love. But it was to be expected since he'd now watched the movie at least ten times, given Nova's habit of watching it multiple times every Christmas.

"If your mum was here, bud, she'd be telling us all about how the boomerang fish and the talking cauliflower are two of her favourite moments, after Rizzo the Rat becoming a frozen popsicle."

Astro babbled around his bottle.

As the music turned darker, the door to the bathroom whipped open. "Are you two watching *The Muppet Christmas Carol* without me?"

With her hair wild, and wearing her ugly brown fleece dressing gown she refused to throw away, Nova looked prettier than ever. He'd never stopped falling in love with her. Every day he felt it more.

"Astro says sorry for the jet lag and wanted to let you sleep in."

When Astro realised his mum was in sight, he began to flail his arms and legs, dropping his bottle. Nova reached for their son and held him over her shoulder, rubbing his back while Astro burped like a sailor. "It's okay, sweetheart," she said, kissing Astro's squishy cheeks. "You can't help it."

She sat down on the sofa next to Presley, and he kissed her softly. "Merry Christmas, Nov."

"Merry Christmas."

"I thought I'd just put this on while we have some tea and wake up before we open gifts. Want me to go back to the beginning?"

"Just to the boomerang fish."

Before he did, he knew there was one gift that just couldn't wait. He tugged the box from the pocket of his joggers and dropped to one knee in front of her.

"Presley," she warned.

But he shook his head. "You told me not to propose

when you were pregnant, and I understood why. And I didn't propose when we were in LA, because that never felt like our place. But this boat has been our place, babe. And I really want to know I'm going to marry you next year because I don't want a life that doesn't have you permanently in it. So, Nova Williams. Given I love you more than life and Oscars, will you please do me the incredible honour of being my wife?"

He popped the box open so she could see the ring, in some random hope that if there was even the slightest doubt in her mind, she'd say yes to the emerald cut diamond surrounded by forest-green garnets in an Art Deco setting.

When he finally looked back at her, her tear-filled eyes were focused on him, not the ring. He couldn't bear the silence. "You've been my best friend since we were kids. I want you to be my best friend forever, babe."

"For real?" Her voice cracked.

"For real." He cupped the back of her neck and kissed her, the ring and Astro between them.

"Of course I'll marry you."

With a racing heart, he slipped the ring from the box and placed it on her finger. It was a little loose, despite his best efforts. "We can get it made a bit smaller."

"It's perfect."

Astro chuckled between them as a small rabbit sang "Good King Wenceslas." Presley grabbed his little fist and kissed it. "This is another of your mum's favourite bits. The wreath toss." He sat back on the sofa, tugging Nova and Astro against his chest.

"Did you really just propose?" she asked quietly, just as Kermit began to sing.

"Yeah, babe. There's magic in the air."

She glanced up at him. "Did you just admit to believing in the magic of Christmas?"

"I think I might."

As if that had been her master plan all along, she grinned. "Good. Now watch, or you're going to miss the skating stunt penguins."

WHO WANTS A FREE NOVELLA?

Thank you so much for reading Jingle Bell Fling. I hope you loved Presley and Nova's story as much as I enjoyed writing it. I'd super appreciate it if you'd take a moment to leave a review if you have time.

Why a canal boat? Because I'm a canal boater. I'm heading out on one soon. Not the Llangollen canal like Nova, because I cruised that one a few years ago. This time I'm off around the Staffordshire Ring over 86 miles and 93 locks.

Please read on for the first chapter in my Love Distilled series set in a family run gin distillery. You're going to love this enemy to lovers, opposites attract romance!

If you'd like another Christmas novella from me, you can get one for FREE by signing up for my newsletter by clicking here!
https://www.subscribepage.com/thegreatestriskfreecopy
Don't forget to double opt-in.

LOVE IN NUMBERS

CHAPTER ONE

Emerson Dyer reached the door of her father's office in their family-run gin distillery. She ran her fingertips across the brass plate with his name on it. He'd regaled her a thousand times with the story of how her mother had hung it when they'd first bought the place. "I miss you, Dad," she murmured before pushing the door open.

The office was still her father's. His raincoat still hung on the back of the door. The Denver Broncos mug she'd gotten him for Father's Day when she was fifteen sat on his desk. Her mind returned to those frantic moments of finding him on the floor two months earlier. Of screaming for her younger brother, Jake, who as master distiller had just started the next batch of Dyer's Medallion gin for the day. She'd frantically dialed 911 and balanced her phone beneath her ear while trying her best to deliver CPR to the man who had loved them so fiercely—who had been there for them ever since the accident happened fifteen years ago, when their mother had died a week after Emerson's fifteenth birthday.

It hadn't been enough.

The doctors had tried to reassure her there was nothing she could have done that would have saved him.

It had been eight weeks yet thinking about that day still had the ability to take her breath away. She'd never get to hear another one of his ridiculous dad jokes, tease him for his vast collection of blue shirts, or plant seeds with him in his greenhouse.

She swallowed deeply and tried to shake the image from her head. She'd barely stepped into his office since then, beyond grabbing the occasional piece of paperwork. Piles of unopened envelopes sat on the desk, and her stomach lurched at the thought of dealing with them. While it was hard to admit it to others, she knew she was overwhelmed. But the letter in her father's will left her with no choice but to step into his shoes, shoes that were impossible to fill.

My darling Emerson, he'd written.

If you are reading this letter, it means I've gone exactly when I was meant to and way sooner than I hoped. I hope you know how proud I am of you. You have been my rock since your mom died, and now I have to ask you to be the glue once more. Jake and Olivia are going to need you more than ever. They'll drift without you. You'll all drift without each other. You have to run the distillery and keep everyone together. You are all each other has got. I have faith in you, Emsie-bobs.

With all my love,

Dad xxx

Her father had never realized it, but his belief in not owing anybody anything had put the family-owned distillery at risk without any savings net or loans to pad their expenses. Ever since their mother had died, her father had been terrified that something unexpected was going to happen to him. And the idea of the three of them being left with a business in debt was more than he could process. As a result, they had been running month to month because her father had remained entrenched in his position.

Every day was a struggle to balance it all.

"Knock, knock." Jake burst through the door, running his hand through his shoulder-length, dark hair that matched her own. She envied the natural waves he'd been blessed with compared to her own pin-straight locks. "Wanted to catch you before you head out to the airport. Have you got the preliminary production schedule for the month?"

"It's on my desk next door. I can't believe it's the start of October already," she replied. "Are you sure you don't want to switch places and go to the liquor awards in my place? You know you love San Francisco."

Jake looked down at his gray jeans with holes in them and his black-and-red plaid shirt. "Not exactly dressed for it. And unless you want to do a twelve-hour production shift every day for the next three days, you're the only one who can go."

Emerson slipped her purse off her shoulder and pulled out the large black bags she brought with her. "I wish Liv felt better so she could go."

At the beginning of June, a violent storm had ravaged the distillery's events hall, leaving it partially roofless and flooded. They had been forced to close it and had done everything they could to accommodate all the weddings they had booked. The tasting room and bar in the main building had the same rustic ambience—red brick, faded wood, and a hint of contemporary in the bar and seating area, but it was designed for something a lot more intimate. Private tours, tastings, even the occasional book club. There had only been so many wedding parties that had been small enough to fit. They'd had to cancel the majority of weddings for the summer months. Losing out on peak season weddings had been ruinous to their cash flow. As damage control, her father, just before he'd died, had offered cancellations without loss of deposits to wedding parties as far out as March the following year, a decision that had exasperated Emerson.

As the distillery's event planner, social media manager, and all-around administrator, Olivia had carried the brunt of informing all the wedding parties about the flood. They'd ranted, sworn at her, and even made threats against Olivia and the company. One groom had taken to stalking Olivia on her personal social media profiles. Dyer's Gin Distillery's social media pages had been flooded with hateful comments, fueling online trolls until it became too much for Liv. The deep depression and frightening levels of anxiety had shown signs of lifting as of late, but it was still too early to expect their youngest sibling to return to work.

"Me too. But we can keep it together until she gets back, right? You starting on Dad's office?" he asked.

"I was going to, but now that I'm here, I don't know if I can face it."

In the past, when she'd thought about how her father would have handed over the reins to the three of them, she'd always imagined it would be at least a decade away and involve a big cake wishing her father a happy retirement. They would cut it on the production floor instead of in the office so everyone could be involved. They'd talk through her plans—the ones that included turning the distillery into a state of the art environmentally friendly masterpiece. He'd have tidied his office, removing the personal debris built up over a lifetime. The pictures of her parents' wedding, of Jake holding a glass of his first distillation, of Olivia's first wedding event, of Emerson's graduation.

But now it was up to her, and she didn't feel even close to being ready. She put her hands on her hips and looked at the piles of papers, the tchotchkes.

Jake threw his arm over her shoulder. "I have faith in you, Em."

Her father's letter had assured her the same. But somehow, she didn't feel as though she *deserved* the faith placed in her.

Four hours later, Emerson was at the airport ready to board. "Ms. Dyer, there was a problem with seating a family together, so with your permission, I'd like to give you an upgrade," said the attendant.

Doing a mental high five, Emerson smiled. "That would be wonderful, thank you."

The flight was only two and a half hours, long enough to have a drink to calm her nerves and perhaps watch a movie—anything to take her mind off the thousands of feet between her butt and the ground. Plus, she fully intended to embrace the time as her first period of enforced relaxation in months. Two and a half hours without calls, interruptions, or emails. Any work could wait until she was safely ensconced in her hotel that evening. She placed her laptop bag in the overhead compartment and slid her purse under the aisle seat in front of her.

"Wine?" asked the flight attendant.

Emerson took a glass from the tray. "Thank you." She took a sip, acidulous flavors exploding on her tongue. It was a touch fruity for her personal tastes, but it was free and available. She switched her cellphone off and let her head fall back, eyes closed, on the headrest. Two and a half perfect hours without being bothered by a soul.

"Excuse me, you're in my seat."

Emerson opened her eyes with a start. A tall man, looking way too handsome for his own good in a fitted navy suit, stared at her like a rather deliciously imperious Clark Kent with his black hair a little on the long side and most definitely ruffled. He looked down at her through glasses that quite possibly made him even hotter.

"I'm sorry." Emerson placed her glass down and pulled the ticket out of her purse. "I was upgraded; they gave me a new ticket as I boarded. Perhaps they made a mistake," she said, wondering why she felt the need to apologize to the ungracious man glaring at her.

She looked at the ticket, then up again at the numbers above the row of seats. 3B. The aisle seat. She was in the right spot. "There must be some mistake," she said, showing him her ticket.

The man growled. It was low and quiet, but it was most definitely a growl. "I so don't need this today," he muttered under his breath, before leaning over her to press the buzzer for the flight attendant.

In spite of his rude behavior, he smelled delicious. Nothing floral. Decidedly woodsy. And the move revealed a shirt that fit his taut frame as if it had been painted on.

"Are you sure you aren't in *A*?" Emerson offered quietly, pointing toward the empty seat next to her, not that the jerk was worth any of her time. But other passengers were looking, and she'd rather fix the problem than continue to cause a scene.

"I never sit by the window," he said, as if that explained everything.

A flight attendant arrived and smiled so hard Emerson's jaw ached at the sight. Perhaps, Emerson thought, she was the only one immune to Mr. Grumpy's style of charm. "How can I help?"

Mr. Grumpy explained. Emerson offered her ticket as proof.

"I see the problem," said the flight attendant, taking a look at both their tickets before placing her hand on Mr. Grumpy's arm. "You've both been given the same seat. It'll just be a moment while I figure this out. Please, take a seat."

Mr. Grumpy looked at her expectantly. Emerson scoffed. He wanted her to move. And while she half expected she'd have to move back to the economy cabin any moment, she wasn't going to make this easy for some smooth-talking idiot. Even if he did have the bluest eyes she'd ever seen.

"It would make more sense for you to move over," Mr. Grumpy said.

Emerson tucked her legs up against the seat. "There's plenty of room for you to get by."

"I can't work if I sit by the window, too much light on my laptop screen," he said, pointedly.

"What, so a woman on a plane can't possibly be wanting to work because...?" She let the words hang.

Mr. Grumpy's jaw twitched, and for a moment, she thought she saw a flicker of his dimple. "That wasn't what I was implying."

"Oh, so you just want it to be more convenient for *you* to work than me?" Damn. She hadn't intended to work, but if she ended up staying in the aisle seat and not back in 34E, she would need to work just to make her point.

Now it was Mr. Grumpy's turn to scoff. His glacial eyes looked toward her glass of wine for a moment, then back at Emerson. "I can only imagine how focused you'll be."

Standing, she quickly realized that there was still a good six inches in height between them. "Are you honestly trying to shame me and my ability to work because of one minuscule glass of wine, taken because I happen to be terrified of flying? Which, by the way, is the reason I don't want to sit next to the goddamn window. First, you get mad because of an administrative error that I did not cause. Then, you invade my personal space to call for assistance...assistance you could have gained had you walked ten feet to the cabin crew. Judgmental *and* rude is really not a good look for you."

Mr. Grumpy raised his hands in mock surrender. "Hmm. That's a lot to tackle in one go. You want me to take them one by one, or—"

"Problem solved," said the flight attendant brightly. "There's another aisle seat that's empty over there." She pointed to the other side of the cabin a few rows back. "Or one of you can take the window. Which would you prefer, Mr. Finch?"

Feeling somewhat embarrassed yet unapologetic over her outburst, Emerson reached for her purse. "Look, I can go back—"

"I'll go," Mr. *Finch* said, although he'd always be Mr. Grumpy to her.

"Thank you," the flight attendant said, casting a look in Emerson's direction, as if she'd been the problem all along. "We're grateful for your cooperation."

Silently seething and mortified, Emerson sat back down.

"Thanks for taking your seat, Ms. Dyer. Mr. Finch, if you'd like to go and take your seat, we'll be departing shortly."

Mr. Grumpy's demeanor shifted. His spine straightened, and his pale eyes glared at Emerson. He spun on his heel and marched up the aisle without another word.

It was the oddest part of their whole encounter.

Emerson raised the wine to her lips, but it tasted sour on

her tongue. The enjoyment taken away by a man she didn't know and shouldn't possibly care about.

In an attempt to reclaim the positive mood she'd been embracing just before Mr. Grumpy's arrival, she forced herself to sip the wine anyway.

But she couldn't resist one last look in his direction, and when she glanced over her shoulder, she found him staring right back at her.

Catch. Power. Recovery.

Catch. Power. Recovery.

Connor Finch focused on the repetition. He kicked his legs, propelling himself forward, turning his head every second stroke to gulp for air. When the end of the pool came into view, he tucked his head and turned, kicking off the edge of the pool to gain momentum.

Catch. Power. Recovery.

His arms burned, muscles already tired from an hour spent in the gym. His mind was empty of any thought other than lap count and form.

The hotel pool was less than ideal, but thankfully it wasn't busy enough to stop him from achieving his goal. Five kilometers. Six days a week.

As he finished the final lap, he reached for the side of the pool, holding tight as he sucked in large gulps of air. While his body screamed for rest, his mind calmed and he savored the sacred moments of peace. He pulled himself from the pool and removed his cap and goggles.

Connor checked his Rolex Submariner, a gift from his father for graduating Harvard with his MBA eight years earlier and joining him at his firm, Finch Liquor Distribution.

Sixty-seven minutes. Damn, he was slipping.

Once he'd showered, he slipped into gray sweats and a T-shirt and returned to his room to get formally dressed. The swim made getting to the event that evening a little tight, but he felt better for the exertion.

His mother had once remarked that he lacked spontaneity. But he'd whittled his routine down to a fine art. Habits were stacked. Performance measured. Results recorded. Why anyone would waste their time without a solid routine was beyond him.

Back in his room, he caught sight of his dark hair in the mirror. He needed a haircut. Taming the ends was an episode in futility. Bristles met his hand as he ran his palm over his jaw.

He dressed in his suit, one custom-made to fit him. With his tall height and swimmer's shoulders, it was hard to find anything off the rack. Deep navy blue. White dress shirt. Silver cuff links that had belonged to his grandfather. Bowtie because it was expected. Black shoes he'd polished to perfection before he'd left home.

With a final check that he had his wallet in his back pocket and his phone and room key in his suit jacket, he stepped out into the hallway. Moments later, he was inside the elevator heading for the ballroom. What were the chances, Connor thought, that the Ms. Dyer he'd met on the aircraft was the one and only Emerson Dyer, CEO of Dyer's Gin?

Donovan Finch, his father, had dreamed of creating an empire like the Bacardi family, a rags-to-riches story. He'd wanted to build a product and establish a world-class distillery and brand. From there, he'd aspired to forge an empire that had global reach.

But over three decades before, Donovan's business partner, Paul Dyer, had screwed him over. Just when the distillery they'd built together was about to open, his business partner pulled the company out from beneath him, leaving him penniless with nothing but a vengeful ambition to become the most successful liquor business in North America.

The previous evening, on the way to the hotel, Connor had looked up the Dyer family as soon as he'd gotten into the cab. His father's constant ranting about the company had piqued Connor's levels of curiosity enough to form a periodic check-in to see how the company was performing. He'd already done a cursory study of Paul Dyer several years before. Dyer's Gin Distillery had never done well enough for Connor to understand why his father's anger had lasted this long. There had been other deals that hadn't worked out over the years, and he doubted his father could remember half of them. Perhaps it was because Dyer's Gin Distillery had been his first major loss, and that made it so...personal.

But now, as Connor studied the liquor market, he could see a shift toward artisanal brands and an opportunity to acquire a portion of the market.

Making Dyer's Gin Distillery a potential target.

Connor's cab-ride search had been about the people, not the numbers. Especially the former operations manager, now CEO, known as Emerson Dyer.

Emerson.

The name suited her, and the thought irritated him.

He'd noticed her as soon as he'd boarded. Attractive, with thick brown hair, her delicate gold earring catching the light from somewhere.

But after the shitty morning he had in argumentative meetings with his Uncle Cameron, the company's Chief Financial Officer, and the evening's pending deadline for a new contract he was working on, he'd just wanted to get seated and get on with his work, so his uncle had one less thing to complain to his father about.

When she'd finally lost her cool, those syrup-brown eyes of hers heated, he'd been distracted...momentarily entertained. She was a flash fire when provoked but was quick to quench it, and he liked it. He'd even considered taking the window seat so he could get to know her a little bit more.

Until he heard the attendant say her name, and he realized who she was.

And while taking his seat was not on the same level as stealing a company, Connor guessed that the genetics of taking whatever you wanted had been passed from father to daughter. He guessed she was headed for the same event he was and wondered how he should handle meeting her again.

A part of him wanted to tell her where she could get off. Ask her whether her father had been able to live with the shady decisions he'd made. A part of him wondered if he should play nice, get to know more about the woman—or rather, get to know more of her distillery. It wasn't unthinkable that Dyer's *could* be their first acquisition of a successful small-batch distillery, once he convinced his father. But perhaps he didn't need to. His father was due to retire, the company becoming Connor's on the first day of January. Perhaps it could be his first decision. No, the first decision was already made—to get rid of his uncle.

And another part of him, a small part he wasn't overly proud of right now, wanted to know a little more about the attractive firecracker who had set him in his place.

To do all but one of those things, he'd need to use some charm. The idea of apologizing flashed in his brain. On the one hand, it felt almost disloyal to his father to apologize to any Dyer. But on the other, as a man who held himself to a high moral standard, he knew he'd been a dick.

Fuck it.

Why was he so concerned about what Emerson Dyer thought?

He shook his head to clear thoughts of the woman from his mind.

The ballroom was filled with tables covered in blue damask cloths with large white floral arrangements in the center. A DJ played gratingly cheery pop songs as servers circulated the room with trays of glasses filled with champagne, and he immediately thought of Emerson again.

She'd been as good as her word. She'd worked damned hard on the flight, poring over spreadsheet after spreadsheet at speeds even he felt were impressive.

His thoughts were restless, and he needed some air before the ceremony began. The ballroom had large doors along one side that appeared to open out to a patio, and he wandered outside. He followed the steps into the lit gardens.

A warm breeze ruffled Connor's hair, blowing through his suit and white dress shirt. The bright lights of the ballroom flickered in his peripheral vision, but for now he simply wanted to breathe.

"Goddamn stupid heels," a voice muttered behind him near the stairs.

The frustration made him smile, and he turned to offer his assistance. All he could see was the top of a chestnut brown updo, and a woman with a heel seemingly stuck in the hem of her full skirt.

"Here," he said, walking to her side. "Take my elbow."

A pair of familiar almond eyes the color of dark maple syrup looked up at him. "You," Emerson said, taking his elbow with a scowl. Her fingers were slender and unadorned, nails short and painted in a pale pink.

"A pleasure to see you again," he said curtly. "Do you always like to make a scene?"

She released the heel from the hem and stood. The black dress was simple, fitted to the waist and falling in voluminous waves to her calves. Only a fool would have missed the way it skimmed her body to perfection.

Her body was trim, her breasts pressed delightfully against the scooping neckline of the dress.

"I didn't make a scene earlier." She appeared to be unaware that her hand was still on his arm. Her eyes were focused on him, and he found that he liked it. "I merely responded to your rude behavior. And lamenting my decision to wear heels with a low hem dress is a wardrobe malfunction, not a scene."

"That sounds a lot like semantics."

"That sounds a lot like avoidance of your role in the earlier matter."

Connor sighed. "You are right. I was in a foul mood when I stepped on the airplane. I apologize for the way I handled finding you in my seat."

Emerson rolled her eyes. "*My* seat."

"I suppose that technically it was our seat. It's called the 'And Stance.' You were in my seat, *and* I was in your seat. Both of us are correct. Both statements are true."

Emerson paused for a moment, then cocked her head slightly. "I can agree with that. But seeing as I was there first and possession being nine-tenths of the law and all that..."

Now Connor grinned. "Are you always this friendly with people you don't know?"

Emerson smiled, and he was taken aback by how it completely changed her face. “In this case, *you* are right. I’m being rude. Sorry. I told my sister, Olivia, I would have been better in flats, but she assured me flats would look stupid with this dress.”

“If I told you that your shoes aren’t what people will be looking at, would that be offensive?” he asked, before mentally kicking himself.

“Urgh. Not offended. And I knew it. I could have saved myself three hours of agony in these torture devices.” She removed her hand from his arm. He felt the loss of the warmth immediately. Perhaps it had been too long since he’d last dated if he was lamenting the loss of Emerson Dyer’s touch. His father would be appalled at what he was thinking. And he loved the way she’d glossed over his compliment without acknowledging it.

“Connor Finch,” he said, offering her his hand. “We got off on the wrong foot. Can I suggest a temporary cessation of hostilities? At least for this evening?”

She reached for his hand, and he could feel the calluses on her palm. “Emerson Dyer. Are we late?”

They both looked to the stairs that had begun to empty of people. Connor reluctantly let go of her hand and checked his watch. “Right on time by my estimate. Not a minute sooner than we need to be.”

He shifted his elbow in her direction for the second time that evening. “To avoid further hem and heel mergers, let me assist you up the stairs.”

Emerson grimaced. “I feel like that’s a good idea.” She reached for him again. He placed his hand over the top of hers. Her skin was soft and warm.

“So, Emerson, what brings you here tonight?” For some reason, he wanted to slow their ascent of the stairs, take a few extra moments to get to know the annoying woman who smelled like summer evenings.

"Oh, you know these things," she said, casually. "Network, socialize, enjoy some overcooked chicken and house white."

"You enjoy overcooked chicken and house white?"

Emerson laughed, and the sound made him grin in response. "Lord, no. But sometimes you've got to eat crap chicken to remind you to enjoy it when it's stuffed and cooked to perfection. You know, when it tastes a little of tart lemon mixed with the smoothness of rich butter all melted together."

Her description made his mouth water. They reached the top of the stairs, and Emerson's hand suddenly flew into the air to wave to someone she knew.

"One second," she said in the direction of the man she had waved at, and Connor felt a twinge of envy. The woman in his presence was quite the dichotomy, and he wanted to know more about her.

He didn't know much beyond her quick temper and her hatred of heels, which actually made her toned calves look delicious. Even her description of chicken had him hanging onto her every word.

"I'm sorry," she said, breaking his curiously errant thoughts. "I've got to go. I was supposed to be seated by now. It was nice talking with you, Connor. I hope you have fun this evening."

And before he had time to say anything in return, she was gone. He smiled as she hurried to her friend with the occasional wobble on the paving stones. She was right, she really didn't look comfortable in heels, but she looked kind of cute trying.

He was just about to step toward the doors to the ballroom when she turned to look at him, a soft smile dancing on her lips.

He held her gaze, as curious about their encounter as he imagined she was.

That was it. His decision made.

Before the night was over, he was going to find out more about the woman.

And her distillery.

And figure out if there was a way to have both.

To find out how it ends, continue reading here in:
Love In Numbers

ABOUT THE AUTHOR

Scarlett Cole is a contemporary romance author that calls both Toronto, Canada and Manchester, England home. A born city dweller, she periodically quashes the urge to live in the country by hiking up a mountain to remind herself that living away from people would terrify the pants off her.

She believes everybody deserves their love story to be told and loves her heroes on the rough and rugged side...and usually tall (because she married one of those 6ft 6" men you read about in romance books!). She's an A-type personality and Scorpio star sign, so good luck getting her to do anything she doesn't want to.

When she isn't writing, she's happy to talk about hot men and expensive shoes while drinking a cold gin and tonic. Don't bring up olives. As far as Scarlett is concerned, they are the devil's food. As long as you don't bring up olives, she's happy to hear from you any time.

ALSO BY SCARLETT COLE

Iron Outlaws MC Series

The Sins We Hide

The Games We Play

The Lies We Tell

The Bonds We Break

The Vows We Keep

Excess All Areas / Sad Fridays Series

One Day Like This

Next Time I Fall

How Good It Was

Love You Like That

Let Me Love You

Love Distilled Series

Love In Numbers

Love In Moments

Love In Secrets

Preload Series

Jordan Reclaimed

Elliott Redeemed

Nikan Rebuilt

Lennon Reborn

The Sweetest Gift

Second Circle Tattoos Series

The Strongest Steel

The Fractured Heart

The Purest Hook

The Darkest Link

The Greatest Risk (Novella)

Love Over Duty Series

Under Fire

Final Siege

Deep Cover

Printed in Great Britain
by Amazon

34857679R00096